Japanese myth beautifully percolates into the lives of the three young people.

—*The Harvard Independent*

Morin's wit can be delicious. Her Tokyo actuality puts Morin several cuts above contemporary American novelists who bash Japan.

— *Canberra Times*

Her most delightful descriptions are of the intrigues in the personal lives of the protagonists.

— *The Harvard Crimson*

Sazzae

J. L. Morin

New York

Harvard Square Editions (HSE), Ltd.

www.HarvardSquareEditions.org

2009

Published in the United States by
Harvard Square Editions (HSE), Ltd.

ISBN 978-0-615-28990-8

Harvard Square Editions web address:
www.harvardsquareeditions.org

Printed in the United States of America

ROUND I

Chapter 1

—————————&)(&—————————

Yellow

Drunken moon. Shintaro slid the paper door shut behind him. He stepped off of the electric porch hanging in moonlight. The great great-grandson of many sat down on a rock alone. He watched the yellow moon, full in silent provocation. The passing generations hadn't left any mark there.

Now I see, there was only one way for Shintaro: The impassionate moon laid down the light. The rock garden hung in its insane law, and there Shintaro's living soul sat in front of the statue of his great-grandfather. Shintaro could hear his grandfather unfolding a futon behind the paper door. Shintaro pretended he was alone.

The ancestor rested on the highest rock in the garden, as he had at the old house. The statue was repulsive. Its squinting eyes and tightly drawn mouth lent an air of accusation to the embellishing folds of stone wrinkles and robes. No matter where Shintaro looked away to — the tiny trees, the darting fish or the foot path — he found himself staring again into the visage of his unyielding forefather. The dead have power over the living. They took everything, and now they would take his grandfather.

The statue stared back. Certain aspects of Shintaro's own face resided in that old stone untouchable's. The high cheekbones, the long eyebrows. But Shintaro told himself that they were nothing alike. His ancestor's teeth had always been clenched, head bowed, ears boxed. As an outsider, an untouchable, he was shrunken into a corporal history of non-existence. Shintaro's ancestor had scraped until he had dug his grave, had never had the pleasure of forgetting his place for a moment, whereas Shintaro had whole days of getting lost in the throngs of the city, of being like everybody else. Of being touchable.

Shintaro sat frozen among the buttons, pockets and loops of his new blue janitor's uniform. In Tokyo, he would be better and stronger than his ancestor. He would grow freely and flower in the stone face of death. Today was the seventh day of his new job. He would work like everybody else and drink coffee with everyone and get paid the same as everyone else. This was good.

He was happy and filled with the strength he needed to continue staring up into the stone face. There was only one way: to sing. The ancestors had not taken away this one consolation. He seized on it to expel the ancestors, to sing to the islands that ruled before ancestors in the superb baritone that was his birthright.

Shintaro took the train to Tokyo. He arrived at the

Ginkgo Leaf Café, and sat with the older janitors. They discussed horseracing. Shintaro said nothing, and thought his own thoughts, *an untouchable must not touch the belongings of royalty*, the legend had said. The young janitors joined them and changed the conversation to guitar strings and amplifiers. Then they all picked up their mops and got to work on the tenth and ninth floors of My King Department Store. They ushered the dust downward floor by floor. Down dust, until their watches struck two.

The janitors didn't have cars, and the subways had stopped running, so it was back to the twelfth floor to roll out the futons. The dingy custodial office of My King Department Store had the loveliest view of night-time Tokyo Shintaro had seen. The other workers slept in the next room. Instead of crawling onto his futon, Shintaro sat on his boss's desk and stared out the window at the lights of Tokyo Tower. He hummed the song his teacher had given him to practice.

At dawn, Shintaro folded his futon. He left the building before the others had woken up. At last he could let himself sing. He walked the streets and sang with the voice of an angel and untouchable feet of clay. He sang the song of the past. The empty streets resounded. He passed through his heritage, was reclaimed, moved freely, was not my friend, not mine, but nomadic. He kept the rhythm with his footsteps, Shintaro. I can still see him, yellow diamond circumscribing other lives.

Chapter 2

―――――――――――ॐ――――――――――――

Blue

A playground. Max looked around, still no one there. In the distance, Tokyo haze hovered over the rows of buildings. Endless wires and terraces and clotheslines. Endless endlessness, and still no one but you, Max.

So. The wind blew through my heart and scattered a name on the path. Look, a name on the path. Hollow names of friends lost and dead. The wind blows them onward, and up into the sky of my heart. Looking into the autumn sky, I see three friends, one of them my younger self, a fledgling, and who am I to say what I wouldn't have done, or whether my fledgling self didn't choose to wander off down another path?

I remember our three souls flying like kites in the air, intertwined, three diamonds of color, flying, falling, entangled in the same tree. Diamond in the rough. Maximilian blue. In the middle of your courtyard, this playground, that night, to ignore the root of your entanglement, that is, despite the cold. A handsome young gentleman skillfully unlearning the guiding

4

principles of *galanterie* as he unzipped his full-length punk leather. Unzipping it further, Max inspected the inside to see if he was bleeding. No.

It was early morning. He was blue, and the sand was wet. Max's head felt like a cotton ball; he was still drunk. In the distance, Tokyo haze hovered over the endless rows of buildings, over the endless poles, wires, terraces and clothes lines, endless endlessness, the sort that is better handled in the wee hours by a sensibility embalmed in gin and tonics. He was ready. Even so, the sight of the city's gray jagged edges crowned in humid fuzz was enough to send Max spinning on his bed of grass at the foot of his naked tree. He gazed at the branches above. As their bare fingers reached bone after bone ever upward into the fog, they also reached downward into the narrowing finitude of his knavish sensibility. He lay looking up at nothing, nothing, and nothing. Any three are beautiful with your back to the world. Yourself, Yourself, and the Holy Ghost. The wind whistled through the trees, *Max*, who knew nothing then. He dreamt looking at the sky.

Max might not have recognized the soul passing through the streets below, or its atonal legend, that a falcon soared high, and despite the arrow vaulting after it, higher still into the recesses of the sky over Japan. Shintaro had heard the story many times, where the pointed body pierced snow-begetting clouds, and as he lent it a tune, he could see his grandfather's eyes narrow with the telling of it. Last night it occurred to Shintaro, that the story had changed, and his grandfather was saying that he didn't have long to live. Shintaro listened to hear what else his grandfather might change this time. "By some trick of the air, the arrow, too, suddenly leapt beyond itself and up into the blankness of the cloud cover. The snow enveloped the two."

"How is it possible?" Shintaro had said.

"Many things are possible," his grandfather always said. He leaned back into the shadows of the porch. Shintaro could no longer see his face. "You are here," said the old man. "I have come across a nomadic soul. Yours is not an unusual destiny, though people may deny it. You wander forward through life encompassing distant times." The yellow diamond circumscribing other lives. Shintaro was made to remember his ancestors' magic that came and went, like the hunting expeditions. They set out in the spring and came back in the summer, fall to winter, the ancestors, the hunt, the falcon, and with them, Shintaro. "But, by some trick of the air, the arrow, too, leapt beyond itself. And lo! the screech as the falcon plummeted into the mountainside."

That a soul should come upon a man is no rare occurrence, whatever they may say. Max stood, having the feeling that something important had either happened in the recent unremembered past, or was about to happen in the near and undiscovered future. He took a step. He was glad. Supremely glad to be cleansed and released like a passenger on a boat, released into the trustingly soft world passing through him prow to stern slowly now as he made his way out of his courtyard and into the alley.

He was looking for a soul. Would it hear his thought waves? *Where have you been?* They both had been here before separately, but everything was misty and new now, and the sun was creeping dimly around the alleys to the atonal tune. Max felt he was getting closer to the baritone voice. This was the street that would take him to where he needed to be. Nowhere near where he was supposed to be. For the moment Max had broken down the greatest barrier between himself and himself, had tumultuously broken with his past, and forgotten about money, for example, which he lost quite a bit of last night.

He did, however, remember that he was above the mass of humanity. He passed two hunchbacked women hosing down the pavement in front of a shop. They bowed and showed their toothy grins. *"Ohayogozaimasu,"* they said.

"Hello," Max said. The women giggled. Max disappeared around the corner. On the main street, everything was glistening and ready for the consumer stampede barely imaginable to a passenger drifting at six a.m. through the empty red taint of dawn.

Chapter 3

---⁊Ͻ ℺---

Red Lady

They belong together, these three, yet alone. I see my third fledgling, the red one, accomplished lady, recovering from the night before when she followed along to the wrong bar where many are finished and none ever started, where, "Who is she?" a man had asked.

"She must be naughty if no one will own up to coming with her," said another man. "Christ. Doesn't anybody know who she came with? Who is this lady?"

"White trash, just like you," said Lois, looking around for someone.

"She sure is pretty."

"I am beautiful."

"How come no one knows her?" one of the men said.

"Must have done some ouch!" said another.

"I am," she insisted.

Lo! Sacred three, etched in the sky of my dead heart where nothing ever comes to pass.

And nothing to suppose it was the wind, a repetition of the air, my yellow friend. Etched like diamonds, Lo! the screech as she plummeted into the mountainside, red, accomplished.

Endless sky, blue with no beginning.

That a nomadic man should come across a nomadic soul is no rare occurrence. Max stood, feeling important. He took a step and recognized this back road. He was trying to remember. He had been here before and had already thought these very thoughts. He grasped at this feeling of *déjà vu* and tried to remember what was next. The sun crept through the alleys.

Somewhere behind the houses, the streets resounded with clay footsteps, the rhythm of Shintaro's past. Max could not make out the angel voice's meaning as it sang of a strange purple sash *lying, snake-like, in the snow next to the falcon, so soft. So fine. It was deep purple, and perfumed. It must have belonged to royalty. It was forbidden. And how he fell to his knees and touched the sash. It was defiled the moment he fell to pick it up, the forbidden sash, so soft, just yesterday,* just now. The people were still in their houses, and Shintaro sang as if out of nowhere, like the sash from the sky. He walked along alone until he ran out of streets.

The siren voice called Max to the brink of nature, a park. The gates of the park were locked, but someone was in there. Max stood in the shadow of the bars. He looked back and forth from the street with its department store and newsstand and other angles and planes, to Shinjuku Gyoen park, flowing green and saw

9

that *he* was behind bars. He pulled himself up the fence. Was on top. Jumped. Landed on all fours. Looked up at free nature through his blond bangs.

The treetops waved in the wind. He laughed from the hollow pit of his washed-out, there-and-back stomach, while all around him, the trees towered and stretched out their bony arms and all around them, the armies of buildings in the very-far-away distance peered fixedly over the edges of the park. He walked downhill through the trees.

By the time he saw the wall of hedges, Max was utterly thirsty. He heard running water, perhaps behind the hedge wall. He climbed through a hole in the hedge, to find another hedge wall, this time without a hole in it. Max walked along it, turned a corner, turned another corner, left, right, left, stopped. A labyrinth of hedges. He looked up at the sky. Where was he? He'd go back to the hole he'd climbed through in the beginning and start again.

He walked along the hedge walls and turned and turned to find more hedge walls. There was the sound of water running beyond the hedge. He could hear it. He had come at last to the center of the labyrinth. Max stood in front of a baroque monument spewing streams of water into the air. It lost the water briefly to the wind, then collected it again in its tiniest and topmost red marble bowl. This bowl overflowed into the larger bowl beneath, which then spilled into a larger and lower tier, and so on down. Though the sun was shining directly into his eyes, he could see a black figure hovering over the rim of the largest marble pool at the base of the red wedding cake. The figure was masked

10

by the dancing tendrils of water. It was making a high-pitched wailing sound.

Max stepped back. It stopped wailing. Its long black hair blew in the wind; it was just there, like one of the trees.

Max took another step backward. He had never seen a ghost.

The black figure shimmered. It stepped back, too.

In Shinjuku Gyoen, the ripples on the surface of the pool collided, overlapped, grew like a confused spirographic picture. The wind fell, and rose again to run rampant through the water and the trees and their black and blond hair struggling with the fist of silence tightening around them.

Chapter 4

-----------&∂)C&-----------

Green

In one languid movement, the ghost's hand reached into its clothing. It produced a slim piece of gold.

Max's eyes swept the bushes urgently for the way out through the hedge wall.

The piece of gold flickered in the wind. Max shielded his eyes. The ghost inhaled deeply, tilted its head back, blew a stream of smoke. The ghost was smoking.

Max exhaled. The ghost was a boy, an incredibly beautiful boy, his body firm and gracefully proportioned, chiseled expression open. His striking nose made his profile impossible to ignore. Max could not take his eyes off of the boy's head, well-shaped under a mop of jet-black hair. The beautiful head stood on a strong neck. Max guessed at the muscles under the boy's shirt, some kind of uniform. Perhaps the boy was the park ranger. Max smiled. The boy's silhouette was still. No matter how long or hard Max stared, the boy did not look up at Max.

Max lit up, too. He smoked and paced and to keep

from staring at the boy, scrutinized the shrubs around the fountain. It was a French formal garden *à la japonaise,* with winding gravel paths and eggshell hedges and triangles of flowers, each with its own color scheme. He blurred his eyes. The gravel paths disappeared and all the colors ran together. A nice copy.

The boy was still there and silent and overtly not noticing Max.

"Ohayogozaimasu." Good morning, Max said into the boy's reflection.

The boy looked up, startled, immediately looked down again. Then whispered almost inaudibly, *"Ohayogozaimasu, gaijinsan."*

Max kept his smile to himself and paced even more.

The boy was looking very hard into the pool now, politely embarrassed and embarrassingly polite as was the custom in Japan.

Max was throwing twigs and leaves into the pool and into Shintaro's reflection, pretending not to watch Max pacing back and forth and throwing leaves. Shintaro had never met a foreigner before. He had heard rumors in his hometown of strange things happening in Tokyo, but none of them had ever happened to him. Until now. Now there was this tall creature with blond hair and, he saw as Max turned, blue eyes. Blue eyes! Max appeared stately under the boy's polite scrutiny. They had finished their cigarettes. The boy ground his into the yellow leaves. Max tossed his into the fountain. They watched it float for a second. It swirled and was consumed. Shintaro was tense. It must seem like he had no business here. And he could not explain. The English language was so evasive. And he certainly couldn't sing in front of a stranger. So, he turned to go.

Max, having dunked his head underwater, could not see that the boy had turned around and walked away, had disappeared into one of the hedge corridors.

Splash.

Shintaro peeked back around the corner. The foreigner was in the fountain! The water toppled down on its head. The foreigner was emptying out its shoes, was tossing them one after the other out onto the grass, was climbing up the fountain. Its blond head looked around for the boy. Shintaro ducked back. His grandfather would never believe this was the outside world for which they left their *buraku* village. Yet, it would be wrong not to seize such an opportunity.

But, he thought, I have already walked away, and my English is so bad. Shintaro looked through the branches at the fountain. The foreigner was floating face down in the pool, arms and legs spread-eagled. Shintaro waited. Almost a minute elapsed. The foreigner did not come up for air. Shintaro began to wonder if it was dead. He waited.

Suddenly, Shintaro was sure it was dead. He ran out of the hedges, and jumped into the pool. He grabbed the back of the black leather jacket, pulled the blond head into the air.

Max spit out a mouthful of water.

Shintaro dropped the head. *Splash.* He got out of the fountain and took off his shoes.

"Come back in," Max said, "It's nice." He swam toward the Japanese boy.

Shintaro stood on the gravel in his bare feet. He was

14

blushing with anger. His eyebrows tight. "We Japanese don't . . . don't swimming in there." The voice was quiet, precise. His voice was soft and low. Despite the circumstances, he was immensely respectful. "And," it said, "I can't swimming."

Max's face dripped. He controlled his desire to laugh and looked very seriously back into the shy, dark face.

Shintaro flinched. His grammar. He should have studied. It would have been impolite not to answer at all. It was impossible to do the right thing. But the foreigner must know that. Shintaro looked into the foreigner's impossible blue eyes to see, but the eyes of the *gaijin* barbarian reflected only the boy's own face, small and distorted, framed in blue irises, framed again in white circles and again in pale skin and blond hair. The blond creature was entirely different. It would not last here. It was here only because the worlds were becoming too full, were overflowing into each other. The blue eyes blinked and stared back at him.

Chapter 5

————————————ॐ————————————

Pinku

The characters bled together into a spot. Lois rubbed the stamp harder. She had simply stopped in at the bar to see if he was still there. The spot still wouldn't come out. She put more soap on the washcloth and rubbed until her hand was red. Wrong bar. She continued rubbing, and felt neither accomplished nor ladylike. She was stamped: bargoer. How professional. How could he have left her there? The shower went cold. She turned the water off. Lois stared into the misty mirror on the wall. She was fair, the most colorless of them all.

Could he have willingly disappeared? That Max. She would have a word with him when she found him again. She put on her earth-red lipstick and her musk and fished through her box of earrings. In the living room she skirted around the stacks of books and the stereo speaker which was overpowered by her neighbor's TV. She looked at the telephone, expecting it not to ring, and tossed her books onto the couch. "Dabie!" a Japanese nuclear family was singing on the

16

TV next door, *Dabie, Dabie Clockit!* Lois knocked on the wall. Her neighbor turned down the volume.

Lois sat down on the couch. But 'Dabie Clocket' went through her head as she reminisced about the night before. He could be in trouble. He wouldn't have left her there at the bar alone like that. She rocked back and forth in her towel and stared out her window. Now this was home. Outside, there were little red roofs and little blue roofs. She blurred the picture and changed the roofs into toy roofs, and the houses into toy houses which enclosed toy people with toy concerns depending on their disguises. The businessman because of business; homework therefore a student. She rocked. Too bad. Too, too bad for the little American out of water, she thought. In the large glass window, the neighbor's TV reflection mutely commented. She rocked and stared through her reflection.

The little fat fruit ladies at the fruit stand gladly relinquished pieces of their pasted-on hearts with their bananas and apples. Black motorbikes buzzed around the narrow streets. The mailman's wooden soul rejoiced at delivering the morning mail. In the background, the black toy bicycles buzzed around the circuit, past the shops and the telephone poles, under the laundry-cluttered balconies, the antennas and signs. One of them was her student's bicycle. The black bicycle, therefore Meiko, dodged through the streets, determined not to suffer as a symbol. Lo watched it disappear behind the houses and then reappear, a larger *kanji,* until the student and her bicycle were almost real.

Lois turned off the tape player. She's brushed her

17

long hair back, tucked in her blouse. She opened the door. "How are you?" she said.

Meiko bowed and took off her shoes. "How are you?" she said.

Fine. "How are you?" Lois repeated.

"How —" Meiko paused, looked at the wall, then smiled triumphantly. "Vely fine. Thank you," she said, and the lesson began. They sat on the couch sipping tea. "Today?" Meiko said, her small frame balanced on the edge of her seat.

"Yes."

"I went to '*Vivre Depaato*'."

"Department Store."

"Department Store and drank a coffee with my fliend."

"Some."

"Some."

"Some coffee."

"Some coffee."

"What did you do today?"

"Today I went to Vivre Department Store and drank some coffee with my fliend."

"What did you drink?"

"I drank some coffee."

"With whom?"

"I drank some coffee with my fliend."

"With your frrrriend?"

"Yes, with my friend."

"Good. What did you buy at Vivre?"

Meiko laughed. "A pinku lipusticku like yours," she said. She was pointing at her mouth.

Lois noticed that the girl was also wearing dangling

earrings, like her own, and red eye shadow also like her own. In fact, Meiko looked quite different today. Her hair was curled. She was sitting up straighter. Next thing Meiko'd be coming in with nightclub stamps on her hands. Lois hid her red nightclub stamp in the couch pillows. "Um." Lois searched for the next question, and struggled to remember her own language. She'd have to make it up as she went along. "Did you have school today?" she said.

Meiko's eyes slipped down to her lap. She smiled. "I skip," she said.

Lois poured two more cups of tea.

The Japanese girl stared at her hands. "I don't want study something."

"I don't want to study anything."

"I don't want to study anything." Meiko blushed.

Lois dangled on the couch. With her stamped hand buried in the pillows like a ticket to nowhere. What did these students want from her?

Meiko was gone. Lois' next student sat on the couch. He answered Lois's questions, at first without hesitation: no, he said, he did not like studying. Why did he take her class? Because. Yes, he didn't know. Did he want to get a better job? His face turned red. He swirled his tea. "It's difficult," he said, and looked up slowly.

Lois stared back, her fingernails embedded in her palms. It was difficult. They said that when they didn't want to answer. It meant the conversation was entering that secret realm, that too-personal-to-go-into-with-a-stranger, -with-a-foreigner, -with-a-*gaijin*, realm.

"What do you mean, 'It's difficult'? In English, nothing is too difficult."

The student shifted in his seat.

It was bright out. Lois saw the toy roofs through the student's reflection. "Very good." Like building the same machine over and over. He paid the six thousand yen, said, "Bye, bye," and she closed the door.

Lois got no satisfaction washing the tea cups with Mick Jagger on the radio. Her friends had taken to ditching her in bars, and she needed a strategy.

Another knock. She opened the door. "How are you?"

"How are you?"

"How are you?"

"HOW ARE YOU?"

Chapter 6

‒‒‒‒‒‒‒‒‒‒‒‒‒‒‒ ℰℭ ‒‒‒‒‒‒‒‒‒‒‒‒‒‒‒

The Walk

The last rays of apricot light evaporated from the *jardins japonais*. It would be a bright day. Max climbed out of the fountain, picked up his leather jacket and rubbed the water out of his hair. He took off his shirt, much to the dismay of the Japanese boy, who was now stepping aside to avoid getting wetter.

"I'm Jack," Max said, and extended his hand.

"I'm Shintaro," the boy said as he reached for the hand. He had never shaken anyone's hand before. It felt strange to touch someone he didn't know. He bowed a little.

"Nice to meet you. *Yoroshiku*," Max said with a deep bow and a court-jesterly sweep of the arm.

Shintaro bowed again.

"So how do we get out of here?"

"Look." Shintaro showed the *gaijin*, the foreigner, the way through the maze. They headed off along a stream toward the hill. They walked. They walked and sometimes talked, and at last Shintaro didn't realize that he was singing. Max slowed. "You sound good, my friend," said Max. Shintaro immediately stopped. Max flopped down under the clouds. Shintaro sat down. Their bodies melted into the grass. The sun climbed higher. A hawk soared overhead. It watched them watching it, and circled. "It's not like Tokyo," Max mumbled.

"It is Tokyo."

The buildings surrounded the park. Max's clothes were almost dry. He closed his eyes. "How old are you?" he asked.

"Twenty-two."

"Really? Me too."

Shintaro's eyes widened. "Really? I thinked . . ."

"Thought."

"I thought your are thirty."

"No, lunkhead. I'm twenty-two."

The hawk circled once more and flew away. Max fell asleep. Shintaro kept watch.

The two wandered through the afternoon. They wandered in their walking and in their talking, often bumping into each other, and dancing around one another. It occured to Shintaro that even though he had lived in Tokyo only for a short time, it was his duty to guide. He was, after all, the Japanese. He watched the tall blond foreigner closely for clues as to which things would be 'fun'. Shintaro glanced sidelong at the foreigner. Max's blue eyes caught his.

The two stopped in front of an electric billboard. Swirling lights, shapes and designs changed from stripes to zigzags to spinning circles until all exploded into a 2-D fireworks. "Wow," Max said.

Shintaro feigned amazement.

The people crossing the street paused, looked from Max to Shintaro to Max and then up at the billboard before continuing on. Both Max and Shintaro realized that they were being watched. Several muscle-bound men, arms crossed in front, stood staring under the billboard. Max and Shintaro straightened up, each counterpointing the other's exquisiteness.

"Do you know Yakuza?" Shintaro asked. "Yakuza is the worst hand in the Japanese card game, *Oicho-Kabu*. The unlucky one get stuck with a set of eight, nine and three, numbers called *Ya, Ku* and *Sa*." The Ya-Ku-Za hand required the most skill at judging opponents and the best luck in order to win. It also was bad luck for any who dared to go against the group. "The Yakuza is Japanese mafia."

Max shrugged. "I feel lucky." He beckoned Shintaro to follow him across the street. They pushed through the door at the bottom of the electric billboard.

They entered the rattling world of the pachinko parlor. Max and Shintaro watched the rows of players, their black wobbling heads zombified in front of the whirring pachinko machines. Shintaro bought a tray of lead balls from the counter up front and was feeding them into one of the machines. "Look here," the Japanese boy said, "keep the balls up." The machine sucked the balls up inside of itself and flung them down behind a glass panel. They came crashing into a jet of air at the bottom, which Shintaro controlled with a red knob. "Understand?" Shintaro said.

"No," Max said.

Ten balls came crashing out of the bottom and rolled into Shintaro's tray. "I won these one," he said, and fed them back into the machine. "You see?"

"Yes. Can I try this machine?" Max poured the balls into the top of the lucky machine. He turned the air jet knob and kept the balls up. "Good player!" Shintaro said, and the winnings came crashing out of the bottom. Max fed them into the top with his free hand, and won more at the bottom. Other players turned to see who was winning. Shintaro laughed. Max turned the knob. They played and played, and finally took their tray of lead balls up to the counter. The man at the cash register weighed the tray and handed Max a receipt. They cashed it in out in the street for a handful of ten thousand yen bills and some change. "That was for money? That's seven hundred and forty three dollars!"

"You are good in math," said Shintaro.

"It's my job."

"The Japanese mafia pay our receipt."

"The Yakuza?"

"Yes. They are the owner of this place."

"Is everything OK?"

"Yes, I think. Do you want play again?"

"Yes, I think."

They selected their machines and played again. They won and cashed out in the street. They walked through the dark tunnel under the tracks to the giant outdoor video screen on top of the Alta Production Company building where mobs of teenage girls in pale spring skirts were saying goodbye to their dates.

The Japanese boy turned toward the foreigner, who was already lost in the gigantic video sequence. "I must go back to home," Shintaro said. He looked awkwardly at his watch. Max started, tore his eyes away from the screen. "It's Saturday." He stared at Shintaro. "We just won. Let's go for a drink."

Shintaro looked away, embarrassed. "But I —" He stared with equal force back at Max.

Max watched the video screen flicker in Shintaro's brown eyes. Shintaro was one of those kinds of people that made Maximilian want to give. What could the boy want? The crowd jolted. Bodies pushed violently past one another, always bowing — sorry, sorry — and pressing onward. "What?" Max said.

"I have no money."

"What do you mean? We won. I have the money right here. Come on." The boy seemed grateful receiving this gift.

The trains will stop running soon, Shintaro was about to say. But the foreigner had solved all problems and was pressing into the crowd to go somewhere. The streets of Kabukicho rang with the low laughter of drunken businessmen, some with red-faced ladies in kimonos, who staggered and clawed and clutched for support, and laughed in those high hysterical tinkles that made their men want more. A thin drizzle fell on everyone.

The rain boiled down from the skies, invisible beyond the red neon glow of Chinese characters on a yellow and blue expanding and contracting digital sign. The crowd thickened into an impenetrable wall. Max imagined himself bouncing through a pachinko machine. He was determined to stay up. The world was closing in on all sides, congealing into a shapeless mass. They breathed.

They numbed themselves to the struggling mob. They expanded and contracted with the strobe-lit sea of black hair and drunken laughter. Max's blond head towered over all the others. Some distant part of him noticed a girl pointing and whispering, *"Gaijin, gaijin!"* A foreigner. He turned his face upward to the needles of rain. Shintaro kept the rhythm. Max's eyes closed, he was oblivious to the tiny motions his body was making to keep him inching forward, to the crowd keeping him from falling obliviously down, he walked with his friend, silent at his shoulder.

Chapter 7

—— ℰ⟩⟨ℰ ——

Islands Illustrious

How the wind blew, oh Muse, as she walked away from her home at a quarter to midnight. The power of heredity went on assuming its hierarchical poses on the platform. The doors closed. Class distinctions were concealed behind the newspapers on the train. Different newspaper, different slogan. Striking through the subway doors, a new crowd broke into an immobility even more equal than the other's, attracting attention from behind newspapers. There were many imperceptible tones in the classical hierarchy, but all agreed, the group came first. There was also a foreigner with a ballerina posture. Lois could not be still, the *gaijin* in her unclassifiable clothing, and had to hold onto something, though there was nothing left to hold onto. On her way to Sazzae, Lois disrupted all aristocratic allocations and fell into someone's lap. They made a space for her to sit down. Trains passed each other going into the metropolis. Otherwise shy boys' eyes met and held onto girls' from behind windows.

Doors opened. Lois followed the crowd out. The crowd broke into different directions, different veins in the all-consuming body of Shinjuku station.

Only a few stragglers continued to walk the flooding streets. The midnight trains were taking everyone else away. Gone was the crowd. The few who were left behind were everywhere assaulted by the sulfurous air pushed up through the gratings, and the jarring screeches of the last trains in a prelude to their fluorescent journeys into the suburbs. She could not miss being everywhere reminded that these people had missed their last chance at returning to the suburbs tonight. She couldn't believe she was staying out again. People were going into the station basement for the night. On the other side of midnight, old leather hands curled into fists against the cold. One hunchback carried a flattened cardboard box on his back down the stairs of the Marunouchi subway line. His beard nearly dragged on the floor. He tried to make his bed with the congregation of untouchables in the network of corridors connecting with My King *Depaato*. They were passing a bottle. His box landed where the bottle would come next. They were used to life outside. This wind was not the kind they disdained. This cold chased in other softer lives. Two virgin teens climbing to the park to cast off their childhood. For a man who, after leaving the baths with his work buddies, had set out in search of a real hotel where he could stay away and look for a place to start all over. They felt the cold and sought warmth.

Lois's heels clicked on the pavement. The trains rumbled beneath. It was raining, and she felt bad. She would have a word with that Max. She tried to control her fear as she passed a dark doorway. She didn't look at it. If she was going to die now, she might as well not know about it. Lois walked along under her umbrella and felt as bad as the people at home always said she was. They had never seen her when she was good. She always wished an opportunity for doing some great good would come along. Then they'd see. But now she had the lever to turn the world upside down, for, she thought, even if I were to do some heroic deed, even if I achieved that golden level of goodness, those bastards in Detroit would yawn and say, so what? They would be jealous, and let her float away. She took shape for them only through her badness, she knew, and braced herself against the wind.

She was glad to have missed the rush-hour people packed in harder and tighter. Safe, wet people passed in trains on the bridge above. The miserable trains hammered them steadily away. The trains moved beyond the mazes of vacant streets and buildings left to courageous walkers and stalkers prowling through their dark empty kingdom.

Companion at his side, Max was excited to be out, for the momentum, and all its random elements. The screeching of the trains ended like a symphony beginning. The rain fell steadily. Shintaro's socks were soaking up all the puddles. It was quiet now. The neon signs had been extinguished. The stragglers were walking in blackness. Down the street they went, past the small park, past the sporting goods store, in this direction, in that, past the four-block-long *Depaato*, dark as a tomb now without its teenagers looking into windows, sauntering down aisles. No one searching for the newest colors, pink, Day-Glo green, searching for the newest oldies, in mirrors, on racks, behind doors and counters, beyond elevators and escalators going up, up higher, farther, faster, sky-rocketing into modernity amidst the crinkling and crunching of paper bags. They went by in their exquisiteness, down dark narrow alleys into the old section. There was one large red lantern overhead and one dimly lit black and white neon sign.

"Here," Max said, and guided Shintaro to an orange linoleum staircase.

Shintaro hung back in the street.

Max stopped halfway down the stairs. "What?"

"I . . . I think it's nothing there."

"It's O.K. I know this place."

They penetrated the darkness of the stairwell. Shintaro flicked his gold lighter, and they cast shadows on the stairs. He saw a narrow wooden door. For all the foreigner's confidence, the Japanese boy could not believe this was where they were going. Could Jack like this place? He knew that this part of Kabukicho was famous for being a Yakuza hangout. Shintaro looked up at the dark street and shivered. It didn't look like there were any other places open.

Chapter 8

―ଚ―

The Noo Sazoo

The door swung open. A big sound exploded into the stairwell. Laughter, talk, talk, talk, Muse. A cloud of smoke poured out of the doorway and ascended the orange linoleum staircase.

Two foreigners stood in the doorway of the dive. A Japanese man appeared between them — "Jacku! Hello!" — nudged the foreigners aside and sauntered out to meet his friend. A foot of black fringe dangled from his extended arm. He captured and embraced Max in one feline motion. They stood face to face. The Japanese man grinned. One tooth was black. "Thank you, Jack," the man said and held out his palm. Max pretended to pay. The Japanese dramatically extended his thin black arms and counted the imaginary bills. Then one arm encircled Max's shoulders. He tossed back his long black hair and escorted Max inside.

Everyone looked up at the door to see who had arrived. They jeered at Max. "His legs are too short," a foreigner with a moustache said to his tablemate. "Not

31

him again," came from a boy slouched in a lounge chair. Max rebuffed their comments with a sweeping stare.

Shintaro stood unflinchingly alone in the shadows out in the stairwell and watched Max disappear into the cloud of smoke. He felt a vacuum open up in his stomach. It occurred to him that he could turn around and leave now if he wanted to. Through the open door, the club invaded his senses. He turned from thought to thought. Wouldn't this be the second night in a row he'd stayed up? He hadn't done that since high school, before the college entrance exams, which he had failed. The door slowly closed in front of him.

It was too wet to wander outside. He wondered what the upstairs of this building was. Offices? Could you get out to the roof? It was probably all locked up. It looked like sleep was out of the question. He stared at the old wooden door and thought of his hometown. The only one left there was his old history teacher. The last time they saw each other, his teacher had announced, Shintaro is the only student in his graduating class who wasn't accepted by a single college. Shintaro had always told himself he didn't care anymore, and look, now he didn't. Ha. The door opened. Max stepped out. "Come on. It's warm and dry in here. It's fine. I know the owner." He held the door open for Shintaro.

Shintaro put his hands in his pockets. The moment he opened the door, all eyes were on him. His well-proportioned silhouette. His turned-up uniform collar was carved into everyone's memory. There were no comments. Gazes crossed and went back to appraising the beautiful boy, his broad shoulders, his languid gait as he plunged into the smoke and through the throng after Max. Conscious of the weight of their stares, Shintaro maintained a downward gaze.

There was an elaborate mirrored bar to lean on and a hand on Shintaro's shoulder. Max was saying something. He stuck his face in front of Shintaro's. "Hey, what do you want to drink?"

Shintaro didn't know what to answer. He was self-conscious despite the fact that he was better dressed than most of the people there. Max followed the boy's gaze to the bartender. "Everything's all right. The owner likes you. He says you can come here anytime, make yourself at home."

Shintaro had seen pictures of clubs like this with mirror squares and velour sofas and sunken lounges. This place seemed more disorderly. Max handed him his drink. Shintaro sipped. He looked around the room. The walls were covered with red graffiti. There were no windows. The door had disappeared.

He had never seen so many species of foreigner in his life. He didn't know there were so many *gaijin* in Tokyo. They were everywhere, sitting on tables, leaning on shoulders, hanging from cigarettes, winding themselves around each other's necks. They must have been models. They all seemed to know each other. Intimately? He watched two blondes and a man with a large moustache flit around the room from one group to the next, animating cigarette holders, scarves and stockings and . . . a see-through blouse! Shintaro's eyes immediately dropped to the floor.

He remembered he still had his uniform on under his clothes. He was hot. He wished he were at the

Ginkgo Leaf Café with everybody else. He looked at his watch. The café had closed over an hour ago. The other janitors were almost done cleaning the ninth floor. Soon they would be finishing off their packs of cigarettes in the Ladies' Room, discussing the races, rolling out the futons and going to sleep. Shintaro was very tired.

He considered the crowd: the mysterious outside world unexpectedly gathered in a claustrophobic interior. Was he a cosmopolite? Each person seemed to be a representative of a different country. He was Japan. It was an honor to have them all mashed together here like atoms.

The see-through blouse's chest bounced past him. Impossible. He couldn't really be here. Jack had brought him. Everything depended on Jack. And what if Jack got bored with him? Left him on his own? Shintaro did not like the idea of being dependent on someone else, especially a *gaijin*, a variable, X. A drink appeared, florescent in his hand. Shintaro gulped. Coughed. Sipped more slowly. Tried to keep up with the back of X's jacket. But X wanted to make the rounds. Establish his territory. He was proceeding from conversation to conversation, and seemed very happy to be back with all his buddies in the deep dark smoky room where everyone was happy to be the one talking to X.

Fine. The stares encroached on Shintaro's space again. He felt a hand groping his shoulder as a middle-aged man steadied himself. Shintaro felt sick. He tilted his head back and breathed deeply. There a new drink in his right hand. He had never drunk before. He had never — and Max's attention was on him again, distracting him, relieving him.

Max pulled Shintaro's arm, "Come on!"

The place to be was on the other side of the room. It was not very far, but they had to stop and say hello, nudge bodies to the side, "Excuse us," and dodge stray hands and spill their drinks and go back to the bar for more. Finally there was a table, or rather a large reel for telephone cable turned on its side. They slid onto two red chairs almost at the same time as two other bodies got up. Shintaro set his drink down and looked around for the lady with the see-through blouse.

Max followed Shintaro's gaze, then surveyed the room. "This is what foreigners like," he said at length. He was smiling. "Do you think it's interesting?"

Shintaro struggled to remain polite. He could don whatever mask a situation called for if it meant saving face for a . . . friend. Like most Japanese, he learned to cover the mistakes of others. Now, as a matter of course, Shintaro offered up the ritualistic expression of trust in his host's goodwill. It was the way a guest and a host struck a bargain. "Yes, interesting." Would Jack understand this adherence to form? But Max had already forgotten about him.

"You can say that again," said a voice from across the table.

Shintaro looked up into the face of a stocky man with a crew cut.

"This place is interesting all right. It's weird. I'm stayin' right here," the man said, "I'm not gettin' up from this chair till dawn. There's too many queers walkin' around here."

Max laughed. "Is this your first time here?"

"First n' last."

"Everybody says that the first time. I bet you'll be back."

"Doubt it."

"Where do you live? I mean, what are you doing in Japan?" Max said.

The man rolled his eyes. "Can't you people think of something new to ask?" He took a sip of whisky. Then another. His face softened. "No, really, umm," he said, "I'm in the U.S. Navy, over at the base in Yukosuka. And I bet you're an English teacher."

"Trader," Max said.

"Really," the Navy man said, "Well, my name's John, and this," he said, and pointed to another hulking crew cut next to him, "is my friend, Bob."

Max started. He hadn't realized there were two of them. They all shook hands.

"Are they American Army?" Shintaro asked.

"Yes," Max said.

The black-toothed owner danced his way over to their table. He ordered them another round of drinks. The owner rested his hand on Max's back, let his fingers slide down Max's arm, and then quickly pressed something into Max's palm.

Shintaro guessed it was a note. A note about him? He tried to get a glimpse of it, but could not lean back far enough.

The crowded room was filling up with more people. Their bodies pressed him so close to the table he could barely move. The sound of their talk, all sounds, flooded his ears, crowded out his own thoughts and beat on his eardrums until he was not sure if he was really there.

Why was the American army here? He knew that they were stationed at a base about an hour away from Tokyo, but it seemed strange that they could want to have anything to do with this place. Shintaro looked around for signs of danger, criminals or spies. Breasts bobbed beneath the mosquito netting fabric. He took another sip of his gin and tonic and decided he was not really here. The owner wasn't spying on him, wasn't handing Max envelopes. They didn't expect him to prove himself. To justify smoking this cigarette, taking a sip of his drink just now, uncrossing his legs, re-crossing them the other way.

Not only were the owner's reports growing in size, they had graduated from business- to book-sized envelopes. People seemed to be watching him. Some were staring outright, others feigning laughter or conversation, but watching out of the corners of their eyes. Shintaro knew. He could see them. The two men leaning against the wall. That man with the moustache. The American soldiers. The group dancing in the corner. That blond woman at the bar. First she laughed loudly, then threw back her bleached head. Then the amusement dissipated for an instant, and she darted a glance at him to find out if he was sitting up straight or listening to Max. The owner was the most watchful. He watched through the mirror behind the bar as he washed out the glasses, and stuffed the envelopes for Max.

Max talked periodically to the owner. Shintaro began reading the graffiti covering the wall. "Go Hawaii blue cheerleader squad," accompanied by a life-sized picture of a girl whose arms reached downward and disappeared into two large pompons. Shintaro stared hard at the pompons. Max was now resealing and shoving the largest envelope yet into a bag under the table.

What was going on here?

The owner stopped mid-sentence and looked at Shintaro.

"Don't worry about him," Max said. "I got some people working on it right now. They'll pick up the information after closing time. Shintaro!" Max said.

Shintaro started. Reluctantly peeled his eyes from the pompons.

"Here." Max held out his arm. He helped the boy stand up. The room spun. A man was taking the table away. Shintaro clung to Max. Max was helping the black-toothed owner carry the table off. Dancers poured into the space where the table had been. They spun and the room spun. Where was his chair?! Had they taken that too? Max's face appeared. Smiling. Always smiling. Shintaro fell forward against Max's chest. "I —" He struggled, "exit."

"No, you can't; there aren't any trains now."

Where was the exit? Shintaro followed the wall and soon found himself back where he had started.

Chapter 9

━━━━━━━━━━━━━━ ❧❧ ━━━━━━━━━━━━━━

Talk, Talk, Talk

The music continued not stopping, and Shintaro raised his head. The red room. He looked around at the red walls throbbing beneath their graffiti. Within the walls were the strange elongated white faces, laughing. How long had he been sitting here? What? What was it? — ah yes, the exit. He turned his head and searched the walls for an opening. Where. Is. The. Exit?

Max's face loomed in front of him and disappeared. There was another glass in his hand. Shintaro's fingers tightened mechanically around it. Not another drink, he thought. Throw it! Yes. I'll throw it.

"It's water," said a soft voice. Shintaro was not sure if the voice came from without or within. It said, "Water." It must be another trick. He'd throw it! "It's water," the soft voice whispered again. "Water." Not an assertion, but a suggestion, penetrating. The muscles in his arm relaxed. Water? He sat back and watched her, felt the heat rise to his face as a soldier came to sit down next to her.

The soldier leaned across the table to Lois. "Where did you meet Jack?" he asked.

She brushed her dark hair back over her shoulders. "At Harvard," she said.

"Harvard. What did you learn at Harvard?"

"That no one could ever know it all anyway. Even the language we build on is mutable, so we slept well at Harvard." June bugs hummed in the cold sunshine and helped her brainstorm on her way to class. Wet autumn leaves, the smell of burning wood, her head buried in the pillows of her single bed.

They had been sitting at the same table in the dining hall at school, she told the soldier, one of those oak banquet tables. She overheard Max bragging about his summer job trading equities. Big deal. That was one of the more obvious things people from Harvard could do. His skin was white. He had blond hair and a scar on his right cheekbone. He was wearing a blue-jean shirt and jeans and tennis shoes. He looked like an inner-city tough, and he talked like a gambler about gambling. He shook his fingers, as if to say, come on, place your bets. He talked about the trading floor: it was a high, it was a low. When you lost, the management let you feel it, and how it was an absolute bore. Everyone was entranced.

Lunch had ended, but they wanted to stay at their banquet table. Except Lois, who had arrived late, and was eating as fast as she could. A senior girl asked Max about women traders. "There aren't many female traders to start with," Max said, "and the ones there are behave kind of strangely."

"In what way?" the senior asked.

He didn't answer. Lois looked up from her lunch.

"They're just strange," he said. He thought about it. "They swear a lot."

Lois almost choked on her salad. *He* swore a lot. "Is that required?" she asked. They laughed.

Max turned his head slowly from their faces to address her question. He would save her grace. "It's," he was saying, "an emotional thing," as his blue eyes met hers. She supposed she must have looked glacial. An emotional thing came across like a wave, and then his eyes said, *No.* No, what? No, don't do it? What did he mean by, *No?* No, I'm not a sexist? Ladies don't belong on the trading floor? It couldn't be her? His eyes had widened. Years later she understood when he married another Jew from Israel.

"Where did you say you first met Jack?" the other soldier asked.

Lois started. "First met? I don't know. A long, long time ago. When we were fourteen."

"Oh."

Lois noticed that Shintaro was finally pressing the glass to his lips. "Go ahead," Lois said, "It's water," said her soft voice.

"Water," the voice whispered again. Water. But a suggestion. His mouth was dry. "It's . . ." the voice persisted. He drank. Water. Yes. He drank it all. "See?" the woman's voice said. Yes. A woman . . . with long, long curls, dark curls, and a beautiful long neck. And a perfect mouth. Shintaro stared into the beautiful face.

It smiled, flash, happy. The face disappeared behind that smile like a Cheshire cat's.

How did she do that?

". . . but we're just transients," the beautiful red

mouth was saying to the American army officer, "just transients, and this is just . . . is just . . . a way station."

Shintaro's eyes did not move from the mouth. Her lilt echoed through Shintaro's ears and resounded around his skull like a tragic song peaking and breaking and dissolving again into its source. "Just transients . . . ients . . . trans. . ." looping and curling back on itself, sounding over again without ever disclosing its meaning. ". . . like a phantom floating through these streets, whittling away at the days . . ." Shintaro followed her long thin fingers as they brushed the dark curls back from her shoulder and exposed a plateau of bare white sand dune swept about by torrents of shadow, unmarked by time, unmarked by man. She shifted the entire white desert, simply tilting her head back. The reaction he felt in his body was undeniable. A look of despair closed over her face. That too was beautiful. Too beautiful. "Counting," the whispering red mouth said, "subtracting, dividing, dissolving, as hope increases loga . . . rhythmic . . . ally. I thought you wanted to live in Paris, Max," she pouted.

Max raised his glass. "A toast." He winked. "To the charming misconceptions of Miss Lane.

Shintaro's fingers stopped tapping out the rhythm of her story. Jack and the woman were friends. The woman's voice went on. He resumed tapping. "And then realizing that I've lost track of what I'm doing and gotten on the wrong train, and then having to admit that I'm not going anywhere, this weekend or next . . . in debt . . . 'cause I'm so . . . ." Shintaro drank his water.

Max struck a match, watched it burn.

"I don't know," she said. "I guess I wouldn't be

42

complaining to you if I weren't sure you'd forget everything I've said by tomorrow."

Max struck another match. "Still," he said, "I form general impressions."

"Nonsense," she said. He didn't remember her. "You're a pretty good storyteller when you're drunk. From your description of all your conquests the other night I concluded that you live 36-hour days."

"Enough artistry."

"It's true. I'm trying to know the truth. It's just that I feel so many different ways, especially when it comes to living in this place."

Max watched the flame as it touched his finger and went out. He wanted something, he thought, but what? He said, "The more you complain about it—"

"Yeah, I heard this last night: the more I'll think about it."

"Right." Max, having discovered long ago that contradicting led to increased involvement, tried his hardest to agree with her, but all he achieved was the realization that he'd already involved himself more than he'd imagined, though he still couldn't remember exactly how they'd met. He became vaguely uncomfortable. "You're right. We have nothing in common." He blew a string of smoke rings.

"O.K., I'm sorry."

Max looked over her head. He took in the room. "This is going to make BIG sense, if we could just analyze it."

"We don't have to analyze it. Look, I really appreciated all the sound advice you gave me last night, like the stuff about taking responsibility for my life and realizing myself, and not doing anything I'd regret, and everything like that. And how I should try to stop thinking for a while. Get out, meet people and do things."

"I said that?"

"That and all kinds of other things that had never occurred to me." She opened her eyes wide, raised one eyebrow.

Not bad, Max thought. "Well, you know," Max said, "it sounds like you really do spend too much time in your apartment. Maybe you should go out more. Get laid."

"I'm an artist. I have to preserve my creative forces. And besides. As this conversation demonstrates, stupidity is contagious."

"So is ugliness."

"That's why I paint."

"Why?"

"I paint because it's the most pointless."

Max stared into his empty glass. "Indeed," he mumbled and looked around for the owner. Where was that Masami when you needed him?

"You guys." She looked at Max and Shintaro. "You run around and talk. You never take anything in. You somedays. You suckers."

"Enough creative forces." Max had to smile, was beginning to remember that he liked her.

"Maggots."

Max patted Shintaro on the back. "He sings."

Shintaro smiled.

"I paint and he sings. And what do you do, Max?"

"I buy and sell, uh, motion."

She laughed. Lit a cigarette. Was silent for a while, smoking. Then looked very soberly back at Max. "I mean, to better yourself. Are you a slug, or are you bettering yourself?"

He straightened up. "Well, you see, when I was born, I bested myself."

"Yuck."

He searched her face. Was she here last night? Would Shintaro be here tomorrow night? Max set his glass down on the table, looked over at Shintaro to make sure the boy wasn't heading for the exit again. No. And he wasn't asleep on the table. He was lost in the face of the woman. Well, Max thought. He picked his drink back up. Well, well. Sipped. Crunched on an ice cube, the beginning of a plan. Hadn't Shintaro spoken of his dream to become a singer? And now Max had found the boy's weakness where he least expected it, Lois. Max looked at Shintaro's almond eyes blinking ever wider like a cartoon character's, intent on drinking in some fantastic vision while the cigarette between his bronze fingers burnt down to the filter. It went out.

Well, let's formally introduce them then. "I'm sorry," Max called to her across the table, "I forgot your name."

She laughed.

"What did you say? Lois Lane?"

"Beat it, Norma Jean." She took a swig of beer.

Max's eyes darted to Shintaro, startled at the sound of the name. Max retorted, *"Max?* Couldn't you come up with a better name than that?"

Shintaro was staring impatiently at Max. Max paused before acknowledging Shintaro.

"Um," Max said slowly, "this is my friend, Shintaro."

"Hi," Lois said.

"Hello," Shintaro said. He bowed slightly without looking at her. Then, to Max: "What?"

"Lo," Max said loudly. "Her name is Lo." He downed Shintaro's water.

The boy looked at the tabletop. Smiled a little. Lo. Hmm. She is Lo. Lo had said, "Hi." She is Lo. Lo.

Chapter 10

─────────────ဆၢ─────────────

The Afterlife

The owner opened the door for the bedazzled three. "Five o'clock!" he yelled.

A shaft of light from the florescent hallway cut across the center of the table. Five o'clock already? Max squinted, looked around, face very pale. Faint lines had begun to appear on his forehead and around his mouth. They altered his appearance. Now it seemed to Shintaro that Max must be around thirty years old, a destabilizing suspicion. Who were these *gaijin*?

Max stretched. Checked his watch: Yes. Five. Leaned over to Shintaro. "Closing time, buddy. Let's go." Shintaro looked around. Go? People were disappearing through the doorway.

The owner turned the music off.

Shintaro's ears continued humming. The American girl pushed her chair back. Lois. Her name was Lois. She stood up. Yes: go. Shintaro pushed his chair back, stood up. The room had become mildly cozy —

47

cigarette butts, someone's scarf, spilled drinks, half drinks with ashes, broken glass and other such memorabilia blanketed all the surfaces.

They delighted in each other, the only ones left in the room, except for the black-toothed Masami and one soldier asleep in the corner. Masami flicked on the lights. Immediately Shintaro spotted the gnarled tattoo on Masami's hand. "Be careful, Jacku," Shintaro whispered. "He is Yakuza."

Max glanced at Masami's tattoo and patted Shintaro on the shoulder. The walls had turned from red to rose. They were different animals in the light. Their eyes flashed. Glasses in hands, they wobbled up to the bar. The cold froze their breath into compact swirls which ascended and diffused.

"Beauty? Come on," Lois was saying as Max stacked the glasses on the bar top, "beauty's in the beholder of the eyes," as she swayed, held onto the bar.

"No, it's not beauty that's in the eyes of the beholder," as he fit another glass into place.

"Ssssemantics. That's what I just said."

"No you didn't."

Yes I did.

No.

Yes.

No.

Remember your promise, Masami whispered to Max, who followed Shintaro, who followed Lois through the doorway. She led them into the stairwell.

"Don't forget!" Masami called after Max.

"It's a very important distinction, Miss Lane," Max said, "but you've missed the —" Max sighed. No point.

She thinks backwards. You can't talk to a woman trying to be a man. She won't listen. It's in her walk.

That look of self-love and self-righteous disdain, so arrogant and condescending, this chauvinistic Max. "Come on Max, how can you take sides when there's no way to know if there's anything at all —" (Her words broke off with each step up the stairs.) "— out there. Beautiful or ugly, black or white, up, down." She coughed. "What makes you think they're anywhere besides in your pretty, rather large head." She stopped talking in order to breathe.

His foot touched the bottom step. He walked upward through the darkness, and out into the street. Into the fog. He was standing in a cloud. He looked down at the mist. His legs ended just below the knees. Max reached his arms out in front of him. His hands disappeared. He put his hands into his pockets, decided not to wander from the doorway after all, swayed back and forth on his heels. The world seemed like a good place today, not too bright. He said, "Eat of the world, woman! for if you spit it back in its face — heh, heh, heh — it'll swallow you whole!" The mists thinned. He saw the doorway to Sazzae behind him, and then they enfolded him again. He was alone in the fog. He heard an echo. "Heh, heh, heh!" Max turned around. The black rectangular stairwell reappeared, as if to back up its statement. Where was she? The black stairwell said, "You're dreaming."

He kept his eyes on the place where the stairwell was reappearing through the fog, a black rectangle. "What?" he asked. There the beautifully shaped head at the bottom of the rectangle. It ascended. Hands appeared, then a waist, thighs, calves, coat flapping in back: Shintaro emerged onto the pavement. He leaned against the wall of the building to the left of the black rectangle and commenced fading in and out of sight behind the undulating fog. He and the black rectangle appeared through the grayness. Silent. Abstract. Waiting.

Then the black rectangle threatened to emit another person. Max muttered, something about hard, brainy women, and drifted off into the mist. But the voice of the black rectangle was sharp and clear in the dampness. It followed him and everywhere pervaded the gray blanket of mist. It spoke slowly, was perhaps coming from the mist itself. It was Lois's voice. "You're drunk!"

"So are you," Max said.

"So?" said a scratchy voice. Max shuddered, faced the rectangle. Could that have been Shintaro?

"So?" she demanded.

Max spun around. "So? so? so?" He was aware of Shintaro against the wall watching secretly out of the corner of his narrow eyes.

"So," the black rectangle said, threatening to usurp them.

"So," Max said.

Lo's face appeared. "You're drunk," she said, as her chest, hips, and hands emerged. She walked slowly to the right of the black rectangle and leaned against the wall. All three stood in the gray fog.

"So are you."

The birds awakened and slowly mounted their chorus in the moment before dawn. From the treetops they could see the morning on the horizon. Shintaro lit a cigarette. Listened to the invisible birds and watched as Max walked toward the wall, put his arm around Lo's shoulders, and drew her off across the street. They remained in sight for a moment, then disappeared. The mists parted. Max and Lo turned around and looked at Shintaro. A sparrow alit on Shintaro's shoulder. The Japanese boy stood plant-like. Ghost-like. Max and Lo disappeared in the mist. The bird chirped. The two reappeared. The coming of the Americans. They were whispering and the bird was whispering and Shintaro heard it all. He watched Max unwrap his jacket, hand Lo the largest of the envelopes. Shintaro gasped. She nodded her head, put it into her handbag. They finished their business and came to lean on the wall next to Shintaro. The little bird hurled himself into the mist with a loud screech.

Lo, Max and Shintaro were each successively about to say something, but each thought better of it and instead simply found some veiled shape to look at: the suggestions of a skyline, the ephemeral bicycles parked at the curb, the disappearing string of yellow plastic flowers poised in the air over the street. Max whistled.

They began to walk. They relied on glimpses of the street and Shintaro's sense of direction. Shintaro stopped. There was a man out there coming closer and closer, shouting out a long, fast string of words that only Shintaro could understand. The man repeated the phrase over and over several times before they could discern his small ragged outline. He pulled a newspaper out of a large bag slung over his shoulder and shouted all the while. Lo looked beyond the newspaper at the man. He was old and thin. Black hair and bones. His stick-like fingers pointed at the characters comprising the headline. Shintaro translated the newspaperman's cries. "Yakuza! Gang! War! Yakuza! Gang! War!"

Max paid the man. Took the paper and stared at the picture. Shintaro pointed out the well-known Yamaken-gumi Yakuza gangster and a new Yakuza clan chief who had escaped from prison. Max tore off the front page and threw the rest into a garbage can. The man's voice rang on, his body annulled by the mist. They laughed at their newspaper, obviously wrong for this was in fact not a new day but merely a continuation of one long, long day that had been going on for time out of mind, lying despondent while humans pushed onward with our millions of fruitless attempts at cutting time's fabric into days, each one successively struggling to refer to, undermine, replace, define and erase the ones before it, each succeeding only in perpetuating its one singular natural error as days blatantly flowed into nights bottled in hours and minutes and seconds to be uncorked later during lunch breaks, tea breaks, and cigarette breaks and for nothing at all as we forget and go on full speed ahead — charge! — and they charged ahead in full career. "Yakuza Arrested." The event was relayed as they rounded the corner of the department store, took the shortcut through the shrine, and ran out onto the boulevard. The newspaper fluttered. There was no stopping now. Down the painted traffic lanes they went blindly at top speed into the cloud. They were shadows. Three faint specters gliding blindly onward against non-traffic.

They stopped. Shinjuku station up ahead, a giant gray square. Other abstractions crept up from the horizon. Tattoos against the sky. They swept the streets, they hurried off to unknown destinations, or waited in sign-post attitudes. They stood to remind the three ephemeral spectators of their individual implications. The light intensified and defined their features. Memory came uninvited, took hold, expanded. Their jobs, their parts in the Tokyoscape. They were ones among the many too many. They stood on the bridge and looked out over the miles of track beneath them. Track after track side by side. Their eyes wandered down the line to the bend. There were no trains in sight. Just a red orb hanging silently above. The wires and planks stretched into nowhere's vanishing point. No rays came from the sun. It hung there, a frozen circle. The purple mist softened the metallic landscape. It looked like rain. There was a distant thunder. Or the echo of thunder, and then no sound. They looked at each other.

"Is that the train?" Lo said.

"No," Max said.

They stood on the bridge and stared again into the red ball. It spilled into the clouds above it.

"Yes it is," Shintaro said.

The train sounded again, like thunder. A light blinked through the fog. The first train. A green Yamanote train coming fast and then shooting under their feet. It disappeared into the invisible tunnel below them as if into a wall, car after rattling green car until its entire body had been consumed, and the beat of the tracks melted again into one distant thunder.

The sky had silently absorbed the liquid sun. It was distributing the colors unjustly across the bigger half of the world. Shintaro threw a pebble down onto the empty tracks. They watched it fall, waited for it to hit the ground, but nothing: it was too small. The party was over. Their faces fully lighted, they tried not to look at each other and said nothing until nothing could not be said. Max coughed. "So, you're sure it's no problem dropping off that apartment application for me?"

"No," Lo said. "It's right near my house."

"Where do *you* live?" Max asked Shintaro.

"Far," said Shintaro.

Chapter 11

───────── ℰ◌ℛ ─────────

Lemmings

Discovered within the confines of humble existence, Max, Lo, and Shintaro disbursed into the utilitarian landscape. The prospect of self-revelation unsettled the three creatures, larger than life and swiftly separating. Back to the margins. They looked over their shoulders, *Goodbye.* How socialized they were after all.

Max held onto the phone number balled up in his pocket. Maybe he'd call Shintaro later. Now the sidewalks were coming up, and they had been discovered, pounding. From whence this need? Each thinking of the other not thinking of the one, dominos.

On Monday, he got up with a mind to work, and he found matching socks, a tie, his briefcase, and generally stuck to instinct. He felt in touch with the markets and eager to trade, even when he saw he was going to be late.

Max changed to the Yamanote line at Ikebukuro and had to ride standing up the whole way. The loudspeaker droned place names, warnings, thank you's. No one on the train spoke. Everyone pretended not to look at anyone else, including the average Japanese curious about the average American, and all looked at Max out of the corners of their eyes.

The average American stared out the window for them. His apparent fascination with the landscape fooled no one. It was enough that he knew they were watching him and that he consent to play. He satisfied their curiosities about the American clothes on the American body, about the American impressions flickering across his face as they whizzed together through the Tokyoscape.

The static cleared, and the loudspeaker announced the next stop, *"Akasaka, Akasaka desu."* The American flowed out of the car like a native. He disappeared as if by magic, only to resurface in the dinner conversations of many households later that evening. But the real Max dodged through the crowd, climbing the stairs, navigating the tangled hallways of the station, until he was at last out. It was hot. He wiped the sweat from his forehead with a handkerchief. Looked at his watch: five a.m. Late again. He put the handkerchief back into his pocket. Walked slowly across the bridge — it was too hot to hurry. Took the apple out of his pocket. He walked along the bridge. A train slid down the tracks below and stopped at the platform. Swish. It soaked up the people, then swish, the doors closed and the platform was empty again. The train disappeared beneath the bridge, right on time: nine-oh-one. He was really going to be late this time. It was too hot, though. He threw the apple core over the railing. Licked his fingers as he glided past the shop windows. Looked into each, not at the stuff inside — it was too small for him — but at the dashing young man, his swiftly passing reflection.

He came to his building, back to abnormal, and took the elevator up. The air conditioning on the trading floor was broken. The big room was empty except for the blipping screens and TV sets. The conference room door was closed, but the CFO's voice penetrated the wall every third sentence or so. The CFO was giving a native trader a Japanese cultural debriefing, in preparation for the American socio-cultural overhaul necessary, Arnie said, for a full understanding of the American economy. Arnie's voice droned on, ". . . while the Japanese, on the other hand, favored the left (or was it right?) side of the brain, and therefore made better arithmeticians, draftsmen, and executors of plans . . ."

The other traders, almost all American, turned around when Max appeared in the doorway. "Hey, how was New York?"

"Great, just got back last night."

"Sure."

They were glad to see him. They needed him.

Max sat down. American interest rates were down, Arnie said. The traders liked to hear the CFO briefings. "Increased investment in U.S. stock. Bonds down point three percent." Max was sitting at Arnie's desk sweating and reading Arnie's *Financial Times*. Arnie enjoyed playing CFO, although the dollar was off and they were long dollars like good Americans. Max traced the column of numbers on the screen with his finger. Down point zero three five cents. He listened to Arnie's strategy. He was ready to make money for the firm.

The market opened. They concentrated on their

screens and traded. By midday, the market had peaked. The phones never stopped ringing. His blood pressure mounted like steel dollars on a magnet. "Way to go, cowboy," the boss said leaning over Max's shoulder. He thought he had trained Arnie better than that. He turned around and glared into Arnie's spectacles. Arnie walked off.

Max's assistant typed the trades into the computer. Max mumbled to her, "I just made some real strong friendships among our yen clients."

She looked at his cynical smile. "I'm sure it's nothing your long-standing reputation won't smooth over," she said. "Uh, with whom did you make friends?"

"All of 'em."

"Good." She picked up the phone. "Joe, it's your wife."

Laughter broke out. "I could never divorce my wife," Joe was saying, "first of all, I love my wife. And secondly, I can't go to bed without tucking my kids in." Joe reached across the desk for the phone.

"I can't go to bed without looking in the refrigerator," Max said.

Joe handed the phone back.

"Did you notice I didn't hang up on your wife this time?" said the assistant.

"Yes, thank you."

"Anyone got five ones?" Max said, eyeing the pile of money in front of Joe. No one answered. "You thieving sluts," said Max.

"Give him those duds," said Joe.

The assistant handed him five ones.

Max pushed them away. "You memorized all the numbers on those ones."

The markets subsided. The assistant picked up her book.

"You read too much," Joe said.

"She's trying to seduce you," said Max. The assistant was reading *The Dehumanization of Art.* Joe read the paper out loud to Max: ". . . Police say in the defendant's testimony he forced her to perform . . ."

"How do you expect me to concentrate?!" said the assistant.

"Sorry, Maggie." Joe went back to reading silently.

She went back to her book.

Joe and Max read the paper silently. "Jack," Joe said, "Read my mind."

"Yemini President Ali Abdullah Saleh has ordered his Northern Yemini forces to observe a ceasefire against his southern enemies," Max scoffed.

Max looked up. "He ordered them to throw down their spears and surrender their stones," he said.

Three o'clock. They re-lived the day. Everyone knew it was a good day for Max. "Let's go for a drink," they said. On his way to get his coat, Max passed The CFO's desk where the phone was still ringing. He picked up the CFO's phone. "We have the info, Arnie: we got the fish officially off the endangered species list. It will be announced next week. Time for a little early fishing. Buy us 100 bullions of the fish stock. Heh, heh, heh. Get it? Fish stock. And, of course, you can tail us."

"Which fish stock?" Max asked. No answer. "Who is this?" The phone went dead. Max looked around to see if Arnie was still on the floor. The others seemed to be going about their business. No wonder Arnie's trades were doing so well. "Just a minute," Max called to the others. He opened the CFO's P&L: one third oil stocks, one third bio-tech, and one third construction. Plenty of room for fish stock. If that was the CFO's next big winner, why not lever up? Max was practiced in following up on Arnie's little pranks. The hand-delivered envelopes with bits of insider info, just to play the competition. Arnie always said you had to keep the other banks in their places if you were going to swim with sharks. It was part of the culture. Most of the trades in the CFO's portfolio had done extremely well. Max hadn't gone fishing since he was a boy, but now he would be watching to see which fish stock Arnie bought over the next few days. No more blind man's bluff. This time he would coattail Arnie's trade.

They all went downstairs together. He looked at the others and wondered if any of them was in on it. It was cool now, but his heart was pumping fast.

"Where do you want to go?" they asked, him.

Out with the paralyzed snobs, he thought. They glided down the street. "That eighty-yen *chuhai* place closed down," Max said.

They chuckled. "How could a place be so unpopular that it couldn't sell grain alcohol for eighty yen?" They would never stop wondering at the whims of Japanese consumerism.

Chapter 12

∽◌◌

Manhole

Lois would have been making money for her company, too, if she had made it to work in the morning. She walked along the bridge at tea time. It was a sunny day. The expressway diminished beneath her black heels like the expressway back in Detroit. Home. Great blue clouds of smoke floated up from the manholes. Home. Perpetual. She was in Tokyo, and she was still in Detroit.

There was no choice. She was just looking for spare parts over here in Tokyo, like a vengeful lover or a dead parent. Her city had rented her out to Tokyo. Tomorrow, it would recall her, recycle her, and pave the streets. Other white people would move to the suburbs. How could Detroit be blacker than before? She was ever white on the outside, Detroit on the inside.

Lo arrived at the company language school. Her boss was teaching her class. It made the boss angry to have to fill in for his own teachers. And yet, so far he'd never refused to pay her for the hour. She sat in the lounge reading his *Tokyo Journal*. She turned to the sports section: more articles about the Detroit Tigers. Tokyo loved the Tigers.

Time. She folded the paper. A new class was waiting for her in the next room. She passed her boss in the corridor. He looked straight ahead.

"Hello class," Lo said. She sat down in the center of the semicircle.

"Hello." A communal whisper.

Lo smiled. They all smiled. "What did you do today?" she asked.

This went over well. They took it as a rhetorical question, which is what it was by now.

"Repeat," Lo said, "What did you do today?"

They repeated.

"Ask him," Lo said to the boy on the far left.

"What did you do today?" the boy on the far left said to the boy next to him. They went around the room. When they got back to the beginning, they substituted "yesterday," and then "tomorrow" and so on, like they did last week, like they had done the week before that, like they would do next week and many times more by the time they fired her.

"Good, ask him," she said.

They laughed and tried to get her attention. They laughed louder and tried signal that Lo's boss had cracked the door ajar behind Lo's chair. Lo listened to one of the girls, who was saying, "I . . . I." Her neighbor quickly helped her. The girl repeated, "I am new today." All the students looked at the floor. Lo turned around and saw her boss staring at her. "Oh. You're new. I thought I recognized you. I'm Lois," Lo said,

"Watashi: Lois." She pointed at her nose as the Japanese do when referring to themselves. She smiled. The class giggled. The new girl bowed and turned redder. The class exercise changed to 'Self-Introduction'.

The door slammed shut.

Lo went back to the office and pretended to read the sports section. The other teachers were talking. The boss giant stepped into the center of the room, ran his hand through his hair, whirled around, saying something semi-urgent in Japanese as he always did when he wanted order in the court. He looked down at all the teachers lounging at the coffee table, whirled around once more, and then alighted on his swivel chair with a thud. He snatched up his pen and began tapping it on the desk.

Lo picked up the phone and tried Max's number. No, they say, he left about an hour ago. She hung up. The other teachers went to their classes. The boss glanced up at Lo, who was reading. Lo turned a page. She reached the end of the paper. Folded it. Looked at her watch. Went back to her classroom and made them laugh.

The class ended. The students gave her presents. This time, she got a giant chocolate bar. She also picked up a florescent pen with a sign on the cap that read, "I am the smart and lovely boy of nice taste, fine clothes, and fashionable disco." Yup, that was her all right. It had a picture on the side of two teens in high school uniforms dancing in synch. Lo thanked her students again for the presents and padded quietly past the boss' office. "Lois!" he said.

"Yes?"

"I've got two other teachers asking me for more

hours, and you can't make it to class. What would you do in my situation?"

She felt a lump rise in her throat. "I don't know. I'm in my situation." She closed the door on his last-chance-buddy stare and slipped out into the street. It was getting dark.

Chapter 13

―――――――――――――ဆၣ―――――――――――――

Generation Gap

Night fell as Shintaro arrived home. He went to his grandfather. "Wait a minute," said Taro. Taro's back was bent over a small table against the wall. His command hovered in the air, though he himself did not look up. The boy waited for a long time. Perhaps his grandfather had forgotten about him. He waited and wondered as he often did whether he must apply the old rules or the new. Should he stand here indefinitely like a foot soldier? He lifted his foot off the *tatami* mat. Waivered. Decided to take a tiny step forward.

Taro turned around.

Shintaro froze. The clock on the wall said midnight. Taro thought Shintaro was six hours late for dinner. Shintaro looked sideways at the table. Taro was absorbed in a mess of nuts and bolts. The oil lamp flickered. It lifted the hard lines of Taro's old face out into space. The dark lines grew into the contours of a terrible mask that struck! . . . and then slunk back into the frail husk of his grandfather, weak, encapsulated in another generation. Until the draft touched the flame a second time, and the mask struck out again. Shintaro hung back, foot off the *tatami*. The dark lines hovered. The candle went out.

Now the old man was all they had ever said he was. The samurai who had disappeared impossibly from the roof of a barrack when his attackers were coming at him from all sides. Wise and terrible master of invention. Taro lit the candle. Took up a thin metal rod, and placed it in a hole in the metal box in front of him. The humming sound began again. Taro continued adding bits and pieces to the gadget.

"What are you making?" Shintaro asked at length, though he knew the old man wouldn't tell him until he was ready.

The humming continued. The old man's fingers twisted and pulled on the knobs. His face remained motionless, a grin fixed there. The humming changed into music and then into words: tomorrow will be partly cloudy with a chance of thundershowers in the evening. Shintaro's eyes widened.

"You see," the old man pronounced, "I have built an oracle. With this small box, I can know the whims of the gods: if tomorrow they will smile on us or drown us, if the barbarians make war or peace with each other, whether I will make my fortune or be your dependent. He braced himself on the table, pushed his hunched back up, walked slowly over to the family altar. He placed the oracle gently in front of the painting of his father and bowed his head in prayer. Silence. The oracle had stopped humming. "When the harvest was bad, the old people would disappear, and no one would inquire after them," Taro said.

Shintaro entered the *tatami* room. They drank green tea. Shintaro was silent. Taro asked if he had ever told Shintaro about the hunt at their ancestral village. Shintaro tried not to think about the two Americans. He studied the lines in Taro's face recounting the story of the hunt for what was forbidden. "Remember, we are untouchables. It is taboo to seek entry into the touchable world. Do not forget what they did to your ancestors."

And lo! the screech as it plummeted into the mountainside, the falcon, as it burrowed into the snow. Shintaro's ancestor and his two trusted friends scaled the icy rock wall, their knives swaying in their belts. "You must remember, we were simple then. Not barbarian, yet we had no need of the comforts you have grown up with. Untouchable life was better for many things. Things that our family has lost today. Truths that have been hidden with our wandering."

"The falcon, grandfather."

"Yes, the kill. Your ancestor ran with the taste of death in his mouth. But it was swiftly vanquished by the beauty of the strange purple sash that lay, snake-like, in the snow where the falcon . . . was not."

They sang the hunt song as they marched back down the trail to their village. The untouchables. They hung the game on the pole at the center of the houses. The ancestor washed at the well, and warmed himself by the fire pit. The stories began: a young girl saved the life of a king with a blade of grass. Then it was the ancestor's turn to tell. He simply unfolded his wonderful sash. The hunters stared. He hung it on the pole with the shiny falcons. What luck. They sang. As if it were alive, the purple sash flew with the singsong on the wind. Its silken skin captured the red and orange fire in its coolness, like the hottest of flames, like a tongue, a flag hailing the cause of the world. Indeed, there were many spirits hovering beyond the halo of fire, and as their number increased, the youths felt their boundlessness. It was the day of remembering dead souls. The sash fluttered triumphantly as if heralding a long-forgotten spirit, perhaps made evil by contemplation of the eternal wrong. The men fell silent. Such a sash could only belong to royalty, and was not for them. Each knew the others' fear, and could answer only with his own. Indeed, the sash had been a woman's pledge, the challenge to a dual. A fought-over woman's aristocratic hand had thrown the purple sash down in the snow: trial by combat. Thus began a bloody battle, red on white, snow stained with blood, sash left on the mountainside.

"But look at you." Taro recognized Shintaro's condition and treated him for fever. Taro ran a cool bath for Shintaro and didn't try to draw him into conversation, preferring to let him revel in it peaceably even though Taro was sure that Shintaro's hopes wouldn't amount to anything more than delirium. He saw his grandson wrapped in his wine-colored bathrobe, and said goodnight.

Shintaro's angel voice sang of how he fell to pick it up, the forbidden sash, so soft, just yesterday, just now. Shintaro sang as if out of nowhere, like the sash from the sky, and he walked up the stairs until he ran out of steps. Shintaro slipped into his bedroom. He unfolded his futon, lay down, closed his eyes, but immediately found himself staring up at the ceiling. There was that face, the beautiful Lois.

ROUND II

Chapter 14

─────────────ॐ─────────────

Trading Room

The ocean is as deep as the imagination. The rare Tiki manta ray knew the passages and holes in the coral reef. He embraced. He let go, he was an arrow, was a sheet. He wrapped himself around an enemy heart. As far as he knew, he was the last meter of his species swimming the ocean. Now it was up to him. In accordance with his personal affinity for hide and seek, the fish floated like a carpet off of the list of endangered species lurking on the sea green desk of a savage politician forty miles above his imagination on the other side of the globe.

Schools of special interest lobbyists were beseeching a phantom legislating power who, with an all-too-complete interest in the proposition, tapped his pen on the desk, and thought, organized crime accounts for three percent of world trade. The lobbyist knew how to slow his pulse. It was one of the more useful things he'd learned in the Yakuza. The manta ray's fate was sealed with one stroke of the diplomatic bic, *voilà.* The cylindrical object was not to be dodged even from the ray's remote haunt.

Max rode his moped through the empty streets to the Ark Mori Building. He straightened his tie on the way up in the elevator. The trading room was half full in its vastness. He sat down at his desk and started wading through economic reports looking for trading ideas. He had a lot of unhedged German telecom stock. Mark-Yen was inordinately high despite poor fundamentals in Germany, and since he wasn't fully in it yet, it looked like a good day to sell D-Marks.

The CFO had a man on the speaker phone. "I'll be in town Wednesday for an interview," the speaker phone barked.

"We don't usually give first interviews in person," Arnie said.

"Arnie, I don't have time for a phone interview," the voice said in almost perfect English. "I'm not asking you to buy the cow. I just want to stop by on Wednesday."

"I'm busy."

"I've been watching your Tiki fish stock trading up. Looks like the sky's the limit, doesn't it, Arnie? But *Gaijin Bank* might have to share the wealth with the new kid on the block."

"See you at ten," Arnie said. He picked up the receiver and slammed it down.

That was it. The name he'd been waiting for. Max typed 'Tiki fish' into his Reuters terminal. "A rare deep-sea ray very high in Omega-3." The article had a

Japanese translation. Max copied the character for Tiki fish and put it into his pocket. He punched in the stock code. Yes, they had opened options trading on Tiki. Time to leverage the bank's position. He called their broker. "I'm working a large order for Tiki puts. What's your market?"

Max looked at the last price that traded and skewed his market to the left. "Twenty, twenty-five, two hundred up."

"Done. I pay twenty-five for two hundred puts."

"I sell two hundred puts at 25."

He was long a lot of Tiki. More traders arrived with food. There was a new trainee in the office, and the skin was rejecting the graft. "What's for breakfast?" Max asked the new trainee.

The trainee searched thorough his wallet, and produced a ten thousand yen bill. "Whatever you want."

"Hey, see that's the shirt Max had on at the tennis match." Joe threw a wad of paper at Max. "Look at all the colors on it! And they made me change because mine didn't qualify as tennis whites!"

"They were kicking sand in your face," Max said.

"Another man castrated," said Maggie. "Back you go!"

Joe threw his Egg McMuffin wrapper into the garbage can Maggie was helping the secretary empty. "Aren't you glad we don't work with a bunch of sexists?" Maggie said.

"This place is disgusting," Max afforded from his seat. He looked across at the gleaming trading room with its blipping green screens and its picture windows.

Amazing the lies you had to tell to keep things running smoothly around here. "Joe, what's going on in the Mark-Yen?"

"The Yen is getting shellacked."

"This looks like the top to me."

"Is that a bet?"

"A hundred dollars."

Joe pretended not to hear.

"OK, fifty." The D-Mark coasted up another basis point against the yen. "Make it that Egg McMuffin," Max said.

Maggie looked at the screen, smiled and shook his hand. "Bet."

The D-Mark froze. They watched it while the trainee made the coffee. It slid almost a big figure. The phones started to ring, and Max didn't get to eat his Egg McMuffin until it was cold.

Preceded by his beer belly, the CFO sauntered off to the bathroom. "That guy's got a keg on tap twenty-four hours," Joe said. Arnie's lap dog scampered over to the trading desk. It sat whining up at them from the floor.

"Whas-a-matter Barney?"

"She's talking her position," Max said. He threw his Egg McMuffin wrapper into the trash can.

They picked up the phones and made prices. The morning wore on; the noise rose. "Talk louder, I can't hear you! What? Five million D-marks you sell against the US dollar at one sixty-nine fifty for September thirty." Max could feel someone standing behind him. "Any questions?" he asked the boss.

"I thought you might have some."

"Yes. Don't you think it's time we increased our

Mark-Yen position? This thing is going back down." Max pulled up the proprietary position. "See?"

"Do it."

He spent the morning watching his profits rise, and the afternoon watching them fall.

"I hope you were out of that trade an hour ago, Jack," said the boss who came to stand in back of Max again. "You're great at picking tops, but when it comes to picking bottoms, you're a —"

"It'll go back up," Max said, and an hour later, it did. Now he could concentrate on more important things. What was the last thing Shintaro had said? Max yawned. Why was he so tired? He rubbed his eyes. The other traders laughed. He looked down at his coke. "Hey, who dosed me?"

A wad of paper skiddled across his desk.

The company supplied sleeping pills for the plane ride between New York and Tokyo so they'd be ready to work when they arrived, not so they'd be able to wipe out the inter-office competition.

"Time to go catch some Z's, buddy," Joe said.

As he tipped out the door, Max slipped a sleeping pill into Joe's coffee.

On a desktop in another part of Tokyo, the strange fish swam around the contours of its tank. The boss ran his tattooed hands along the tank and peered in at the ray's soft flesh. He couldn't read the American newspaper, but he could see that the fish had made it through customs. The bans had been lifted. He had bought his fish stock in time, and his $50 million was now $300 million. "I should have bought more. If only the conceited American hadn't become suspicious. Never mind. I got rid of those puts, and I'll have the last fish."

Chapter 15

Time Passes Successfully

Lois opened her mailbox. She had checked every day, and now a letter from America. She remembered her existence prior to this half-life.

Up the four flights of stairs and into her apartment and onto the couch she went thinking, America, and how she'd thought she'd never want to go back there. But now, now she'd give up her . . . her what? to be floating around in that wombly darkness on the other side of the world.

In a bar. In Detroit. Listening to a live band. Driving a big car. To the clubs to get paid. In the land of plenty, America, America, tizz a fee. The big Us. But she was stranded here with no money. She read the letter in her lap. It was from one of her roommates from college who wanted to know if the gossip she heard about Lo hanging out with an underworld spy was true. Maybe Lois had exaggerated in her last letter, but it would be a shame to let them down now that she had started this rumor so neatly herself. Lo read on. Her roommates wanted to know more about the debonair young man intent on concealing his true identity. Lois stared out the window at the red roofs and the blue roofs. The phone rang. She touched it, waited for the second ring, answered. This was not America. Someone prattled to her in Japanese. "Do you speak English?" she said. No change. "Please speak more slowly," she said in Japanese. She put down the receiver, closed her eyes and stared hard into the blackness.

The perfect setting for a monster movie. She saw the long-awaited Great Tokyo Earthquake wiping out all the people and buildings in and around Tokyo. Flying pillars and slabs of concrete. All the subway trains stopped, and everybody was buried alive, the earth opened up outside her window and swallowed her house.

She imagined she felt a tremor. Maybe it was someone's mispronunciation on the TV next door. The shaking sound continued. It really was a tremor. The eighteenth since she'd been here. She searched for a distraction, the newspaper, grabbed it, read randomly. ". . . due to the high polygamy threshold of the lek-breeding grouse . . ." If the male's benefits gained from a polygamous relationship were greater than the costs incurred, then polygamy evolved. The windows rattled. She wondered what her polygamy threshold was, but the article didn't say how to figure out your own; there were liabilities to be avoided, and surely some diseases waiting. The dishes clattered. Her eyes read on unattended by her consciousness, which had reached her earth tremor threshold. A tiny bug, tinier than a cell, swam with the whale-like red and white cells through her blood stream. It was the size of nothing. Just a slice of DNA. RNA. CIA. A secret code. A message. A program from the Devil that had found its mark in her body computer. The bug adhered to the wall of a red blood cell. Its enzymes ate away at the cell wall and it swiveled into the gelatinous cytoplasmic Eden. Now, slithering through the darkness of the cell's interior, this tablet, space voyager, casket delivered its evil code — "Be as the Gods" — to the nucleus, which welcomed the news, and duplicated it and spread it like a blanket. Death by falling buildings, it didn't really matter when she started to think about it. The last time she was in an earth tremor, it woke her up from a dream that she was in her kitchen where the pot roast had caught on fire. They were kids. It was a recurring dream. A huge laser beam of light shot out of the pot straight up to the ceiling where it burnt a hole. Max held a pot lid over the beam, deflecting the light onto the refrigerator. It started burning a hole there too, so the two of them ran around the kitchen with pot lids trying to deflect the beam of light, which was angling everywhere and burning everything anyway and drawing a more and more complex picture of a spider's web.

She was not shaking, regardless of the walls, and went on reading. It seemed that there was a virus whose existence depended on getting from one cow to another. It entered the brain of a certain type of ant that ate cow dung. The virus reprogrammed the ant's genetic material to make the ant climb to the tip of a blade of grass and go into suspended animation waiting for the cow to come along and eat it.

When the earth stopped shaking, she was in the

process of setting up her easel and canvas on the terrace, was looking around for a subject. Lo stared out at the bleak landscape and realized that there was really only one subject out there: the red roofs and the blue roofs. Or maybe one roof. Red or blue? They were all equal. Her eyes drifted toward the horizon. Without knowing it, she had set up her easel and canvas, had squeezed out three colors onto the palette, had begun painting.

She filled one corner with tiny, unsure strokes, and then another and another and the last. By the time she thought of approaching the center, it was clear that everything was going to be hopelessly out of proportion. She had to change almost everything. She should be thinking in terms of an overall sketch at first, not all this detail. Her strokes grew in size and sureness, touched on different areas of the canvas almost at random. They took on a rhythm of their own. The tremor ended.

A story weaved itself in her head. It was an old story that had suggested itself time and again, and it guided her hand through the hour, directed her as to how to paint it. It was about Maximilian, of course, the story of a kingdom in a valley, a place she'd always known. First she covered the whole canvas with the valleys, and this was the general, the background. Paint the valleys black, the voice told her, as in Modigliani, as in plumbing. The black valleys were so low down in the depths of everything that daylight never touched them. They peered up through holes in the color. As if by accident, the background pierced the images painted over it and jumped into her eye, Max, coming out everywhere. The song went on. The images were the mountains you made out of the things the painting was going to be about, and those mountains rose up out of the valleys of darkness and into a rainbow of color and shadow and definition, like mountains thrust up into the divine eye, like knives, the mountains. And these mountains of color conversed with each other only through silent gravitation and tension, their peaks, points in chorus, as if to spite time, to make the one plastic point. The painting leapt from the canvas, and she had executed an idea. The blood of execution staining her hands.

Her strokes became small and definite. She stared at the canvas. The voice went on revealing itself to her. It was the story of a sad queen in a land far, far away across the sea. She lit a cigarette, blew a stream of smoke. It hurled itself at the canvas and exploded against the surface. The smoke cleared. The colors began to make sense. The first "mountain" erupting out of the darkness was a lady in a white dress, in contrast to the dark Maximilian, perhaps only existing because of him. You couldn't really tell she was a lady, but she was white. And there was a dark square at the white lady's feet; it was the gate, the stairwell, and it was also a man. Maximilian, in the story at least. And in front of the dark gate that was Maximilian was an empty garden. The gate was supposed to lead into the garden, but now that she had stopped to look at it, it didn't come across that way; instead, the three were stacked up like a totem, the garden on the bottom, the queen on top, and the black doorway that was Maximilian in the middle. Everything was disconnected. On non-intersecting planes. And there didn't seem to be any way to connect them, even though she'd done it many times before in other paintings. For some reason, this time, they were all disconnected.

She listened to the voice tell about never seeing Maximilian again, except through the veil of dreams. She watched her fingers wrapped around the brush painting the colors to the soft voice of the white queen.

Cover the canvas with the general blackness, the queen seemed to be saying. *The general valleys, the depths, the crags and pits, the bases and foundations of all that is wondrous and powerful. From these depths, the great will climb. Great people, great actions, again the Sisyphans will stand unstraining and free, if only briefly, on the mountaintops. Draw lines from one to the next and describe the picture of history and the map of life. Paint my Maximilian, a plastic memory, the embodiment of his greatest self embossed in death, his hand still warm on the breast of his white-widow queen, already nothing but a vessel. My queenly body thins into a dissemblance, chips away and cascades piece by white porcelain piece into unrememberedness, the dark background. How lovely your painting is.*

Lo ran her black fingers through her dark hair. She painted the perimeter of the square. It didn't seem to matter which side she straightened; the black square that was Maximilian never looked like a perfect square. One side was always out of proportion with the others no matter how she worked to justify its faults. And it was always getting bigger and bigger. It ate away at the canvas and poisoned the song of the poor white queen writhing in pain and thrashing at the black slaying square that had delivered this baneful package of mortality wrapped tightly around the neck of her still-originating form. *The black slayer delivered the punch line and even now laughs at my noble self, a joke, damned to believe myself alive.*

So the black square would have to remain imperfect. The tea kettle whistled. She washed out the brush, and poured the tea. She looked at her canvas. At this moment, it was beautiful. She was still inside of it, had not yet separated herself. But how angry she felt, as if she herself were the queen, torn from Maximilian's side. She put down her teacup. Time was running out. She hurried to paint a golden chalice overflowing with wine, and the white queen's delicate white hand to hold it. There. She would sip the days as they filled her cup. She tried to set down her brush, but the square had gotten into the chalice, and the more she tried to get it out, the larger the square grew. Though the queen had guarded it with all her might from the slayer, she could not save her golden chalice. It ran black with a bitter drink of time to which she had become all too addicted and could not sip slowly.

The story continued telling itself to her, saying, *Try as you will to let the mountains seal off the craggy depths so that only their peaks can bask in the sun, it cannot be, for their time has already come, and the darkness already creeps into the heart of each thing and reclaims it, from the inside out.* A hole had gotten into the queen's heart. Lo continued painting at the edges of the hole. Now the white shape looked more like a doughnut than a queen. The sick queen propped herself up against the gate — the black square, Maximilian — so large now that it had almost pushed her out of the picture entirely. She moaned and struggled and aspired to have her place in the world and unwittingly died of birth. She pushed on the doorway and ranted, *I have striven to wield a power beyond life itself!*

The black square pushed the queen's elongating body to the edge of the canvas.

"A power which can remain, remain, Remain!" She was very thin now. Her chalice had fallen from her hand. The louder she screamed, the smaller her voice became. Lo strained to hear the words behind the quickening rhythm of her screams.

"No! Listen! My pregnancy is long and sleepless and full of nothing . . . but once I have brought my monument — mine — into the world, I will go freely. Only then. I will be free, to go peacefully to my garden, and be with you, Maximilian, forever."

Lo lit a cigarette. Stared at the queen. Blew the smoke. It exploded into a mushroom cloud against the ectoplasmic image, curled and reshaped the canvas until at last she saw how time connected the gate to the queen, and the queen to the garden . . . *and time's dark drink will creep into the heart of each thing and reclaim it from the inside out.*

But the white queen objected. *No! You have no idea of my situation! You are no artist who cannot herself sympathize with her subject. I am your queen! I demand that you spare me!*

Lois picked up her brush, put it down. Picked it up. Put it down. Better to suffer the illusion indefinitely, or die twice? She picked up the brush.

You are blind!

Tableaux, currency of the next century. She took the painting inside and leaned it against the wall by the window.

Chapter 16

─────────────────8003─────────────────

The Scene of the Crime

The lights in the audition hall went down. Maximilian waved at a man in the front row, but now in the dark, Kato's head looked like every other. Maximilian cruised down the aisle, walked up in front of the stage, turned around and faced the audience.

"Jaku! Jaku! Heeah! Come ovah heeah!" Kato shouted and waved his arms.

Maximilian squeezed into the second row and sat down behind the businessmen, two of whom seemed somewhat familiar. Kato's mergers-and-acquisitions friends. Maximilian tried and failed to remember their names. He said, *"Konbanwa,"* and smiled extra hard at the two familiar men and thanked them generally for this rare invitation to witness a record company audition. It hadn't been easy to persuade them to invite him. The two men smiled back extra hard in symmetry from their square suit jackets. "Good evening, good evening," they said. They had on gray pants.

Maximilian tucked in his shirt. *"Konbanwa,"* he said.

The director pranced back and forth across the stage and shouted a stream into his megaphone. He did not look at Kato's group. He seemed uninterested in Kato's esteemed American guest.

Maximilian tried to get comfortable in the small seat. He resolved himself into a half-fetal position. His knees dug into the seat cushion in front of him. Now the director had stopped shouting, was leaning against an amplifier. Now he let the megaphone rest on his knee. His eyes wandered around the auditorium, everywhere, except to the place where Kato's group was sitting with the American. That must be the guy who arranged for my invitation, Maximilian thought. The performers shuffled out onto the stage. The director picked up his megaphone systematically to raise a little hell. He was the lieutenant. He made the auditioners scramble into a line beginning with the tallest and ending with the shortest. Maximilian searched the line for his next idol, but didn't see any real *kamikaze*.

Kato leaned over three of his business associates to Maximilian. "They are want to become a teen idol," Kato said and laughed loudly. The three men laughed, too. Kato laughed louder, but, seeing Maximilian's face unmoved, added, "Please excuse my bad English."

"Teen idols, huh? Jesus, none of them looks older than twelve," Maximilian said.

"Yes. They are Japanese. They are about twenty, but not very professional. Look at that girl's feet."

Maximilian followed Kato's gaze to an awkward girl's feet under the banquet table. "She looks like she's downshifting," Maximilian said. He looked around the audition hall. "Who is that man with the megaphone?"

"Ah!" They all laughed. "That's the man who is also from the record copolation," Kato said, "Matsuisan. He works with us to choose the singers who will receive the record copolation promotion to become teen idol"

"The record company decides who will become a star?"

"*So.* Yes, that's collect."

They fell silent. The megaphone man pointed, shouted, posed. Still, he did not look in Maximilian's direction. "What about independent bands?" Maximilian asked.

The businessmen looked into each other's eyes. "Independento?" they asked each other.

"Yes," Maximilian said, "Singers who do not come to this audition."

"No no. He can sing in the small club, but he cannot become a stah! And when the singer is chosen by a record company, he must train very hard for many month to sing the song."

"What song?"

"The songwriter's song."

"Who is the songwriter?" Maximilian asked.

"He is the smart businessman."

"I see."

"He write the song for the record copolation."

"Really? And can't the singer ever make his own songs?"

"There are a . . . a-handful-of." Kato looked at his colleagues. They laughed. They had learned this expression in their English class that afternoon.

"A handful of songwriters write the songs. They are the salarymen. And the singers will become a salarymen too.

They get a pay, about one hundred thousand yen per month at the start."

"Oh."

Kato, all company pride, sat back in his seat.

"One hundred thousand yen?" Maximilian asked.

"So. Yes. One hundred thousand yen."

Maximilian could make that in a matter of minutes. So now he was making more than the 'stahs'.

Onstage, the tallest, gawkiest girl got pushed forward by her shy competitors. The girl covered her mouth with her hand, laughed nervously. Now the man shouted at her with his megaphone. She walked up to the microphone, and the music started. She took a deep breath, pressed her lips to the microphone, exhaled. But all that came out were tiny bells of laughter.

The music stopped. A monotonous flow exuded from the megaphone. The girl bowed. The megaphone man bowed. She cried, bowed again, scampered off the stage. A boy stepped up to the microphone.

Maximilian leaned forward. That boy looked awfully familiar. His gestures, his mannerisms bore a striking resemblance to Shintaro. The boy looked up. No, Maximilian thought, Shintaro was much better looking.

In truth, however, Maximilian had already forgotten the details of Shintaro's appearance. What the Japanese boy's voice sounded like, what kind of clothes he wore, his mannerisms. Maximilian searched the line on the stage, but could not find anyone as perfect as Shintaro for the part. Maximilian thought, if I can pull this off, Shintaro will be indebted forever. I can pay for singing lessons. Then again, Shintaro would have to put up with far too much mediocrity. Maximilian had seen his share of teen idol posters, silly teen idol T-shirts and baseball cards in Harajuku street stands. As far as he was concerned, the teen idol business was devoted strictly to the production of trash.

Still. Maximilian's eyes traveled up and down the line on the stage. He kept catching glimpses of a particularly Shintaresque chin or posture, Shintaro shoulders or eyes. Teen idolship might not be such a bad scam. Pretty much anyone could become a teen idol. Anyone with minor talent and good looks. Anyone with a silver-tongued manager, and a teacher persistent enough to train out that long-cultivated Japanese teen shyness, and to instill in its place a healthy love of money. Anyone could win the lottery. Anyone who bought a ticket. The executive decision was made: Shintaro would win that split-second of fame.

By now the boy had finished singing and was stepping down into the audience. No, Maximilian was thinking as the boy glided past, he was not like Shintaro. The boy's swaying body dipped behind the megaphoneman and disappeared through the door. Another female singer stepped up to the microphone. "Mm," Kato mumbled. He leaned toward Maximilian. "This one is not so pretty. The pretty girl has the better chance to become the teen idol."

"Hmm?" Maximilian said, and turned to Kato. "Oh. Yes, she is very pretty."

Kato's eyebrows ascended to his hairline.

The music started. She sang. She seemed to be singing a song entirely different from the music that was playing. Her liquid voice trilled to the top of its range and hit high C. Kato's glasses cracked.

Maximilian laughed.

"Occupational hazardo." Kato removed his glasses. "Too much like classic," he said. "We want a pop." The next girl came forward. The four businessmen never stopped talking and laughing among themselves. Maximilian shrank down in his seat. The curtains closed. Maximilian's eyes closed. Kato tried to inform the *gaijin* that it would be a couple minutes before the stage was cleared for the dancing auditions. Maximilian barely heard him. Someone coughed. A pamphlet fluttered to the floor. Maximilian fell asleep.

An olive-skin curtain peeled back in his dream to reveal an old-world feudal village set. A young boy sat on top of a half-circle bridge almost naked. He was hidden by the railing. His feet stretched to touch the imaginary water beneath, his chest muscles flexed. His arms were wrapped around the overhead railing from which a kimono also hung gracefully unoccupied in the wind. The music started: "Pineapple loves peachfuzzy in her mocha tea," a popular song in the sixties. "I bear secret promises of love," the boy's voice sang, "Take me to your leader." The singer was Shintaro . . . you could tell by the bridge. He would speak. Time's wrinkles opened into the pool of desire, every thought a nerve ending which bid thee farewell across the threshold of frustrated ambition. The dream expired.

Stage lights went down, auditorium lights came up. A hush spread across the room, then came the soft chatter of the audience, the judges, the singers. Maximilian tried not to notice that someone was shaking his shoulder. Kato. Maximilian's eyes opened. "Would you like whisky?" Kato asked, "Jaku, whisky?"

"Is it over?" he said.

"Yeah, ovah. The result will be next week."

"Oh. Do tell me."

"Of course."

The megaphone man came over. Maximilian bowed. "Thanks to all of you for inviting me."

"It's my pleasure," the megaphone man said. "Say hello to Arnie. Next time he come with you."

"Yes," Maximilian said.

Kato said, "Let's go whisky."

Maximilian smiled. "Let's go whisky."

The megaphoneman followed without saying anything. The judges crowded around their *gaijin* and exited stage left.

Into the whisky bar. "Please, a little more water," Kato begged the girl in his lap.

"But your English is better when you drink," she coquettishly argued. "And look at the *gaijin*. His glass is orangie; he can drink so much more than you."

Kato's face could not have been any redder. He took the glass from her and downed it in one swallow. Everyone laughed.

"The American is the professional drinker," one of the judges pointed out.

"He have more blood than we do," said another judge.

"I think so too. (I can't believe I said in English!)" said another.

"You are drunk."

"I can speak to Jack! Do you like the Japanese singer?"

Maximilian smiled. He played with his chopsticks to prolong the silence. Time to close the deal, Max thought, still saying nothing.

Soon he had them begging for more information. "Maybe Jack sees a better singer in America."

"No," Maximilian said, "not in America."

The judges looked at each other. The hostess filled all the glasses. Sat down next to Maximilian, rearranged his placemat.

A fat judge broke the silence. "Not in America? Where, Jack, is the better singers?"

A thin judge answered. "It must be in Europe."

Kato added, "There are many, many *gaijin* heeah in Tokyo."

The thin judge said, *"So desu ne,* but they can't understand Japanese, and can't be a teen idol."

"No," Maximilian said, "not a *gaijin.*"

"Rearry?" said the fat judge.

The thin judge repeated, "Really? How did you met him?"

"Well let's see. First of all, he is a Japanese boy. Very handsome. We met at a good friend's company party."

"Ahhh. I see." They shook their heads in agreement.

"The boy's grandfather was a famous, uh, scientist," Maximilian said, "and his mother knows everything about the stage."

"Does he practice singing?"

"Does he practice? Are you kidding? Every day, this boy wakes up before dawn and goes to Shinjuku Gyoen

Park to practice." Maximilian started to pour himself another drink.

The hostess took the bottle away from him and finished pouring his drink. "It's my job, thank you!" She tried to add some water to his whisky. Maximilian stopped her with an icy look. He took a swig of whisky, swished it around, swallowed. Maximilian's eyes successively met those of the four judges. He said, "This boy Shintaro fills his mouth with marbles, and then tilts his head back to practice singing." Maximilian gargled the remainder of his whisky to demonstrate the principle.

"He sound like the kind who thinks teen idol is a game," said the thin judge.

"No, it's scientific," Maximilian said, "but maybe he's too clever for you. His I.Q. is very high. Tokyo University asked him to enter a couple years ago, but he refused. He loves singing so much."

All eyebrows rose. "Turning down Tokyo University? That's good for marketing." The hostess called over two more hostesses who begged Maximilian to repeat the story of the next great teen idol. The table was full.

"He is very serious, very handsome, and has the best voice in Japan. And. His image is the kind that makes the best teen idol," Maximilian continued.

The hostess translated Maximilian's speech simultaneously in a low whisper to the two non-English-speaking hostesses.

The fat judge said, "What did you say his name is?"

"We call him . . . uh . . . 'Tomorrow'," Maximilian said.

"Please bring him to this club," said one hostess.

"I don't know," Maximilian said. "He doesn't drink. Like I said, a teen idol must not only be handsome, but also innocent. Someone teens can respect and, uh, trust. A role model."

"*So desu ne.* I told you all so just today," said Katosan.

The judges agreed. "*So desu ne.*"

"This boy has the image that makes the best idol. He is so gentle that birds come and land on his shoulder."

The thin judge laughed.

Kato quieted the thin judge and said, "No. I think I have heard of him now."

"Anyway, forget it," Maximilian said. "He's so busy. I don't like to call him too often, unless it's . . . important . . . and definite."

"Today was the last day of the audition," said the thin judge.

"Yes. And you probably found the most beautiful and talented idols already." Maximilian went silent again.

The thin judge said, "Hmm."

"Hmm," said the fat judge.

The women giggled. They all looked at the megaphoneman. "Hmm," he said at last. "*So desu, ne.* He can audition with the finalists. Jaku, please to call him."

"For you, no problem."

The salarymen bowed. "Thank you," said the megaphone man. "Now let's go Turkish bath!"

Chapter 17

───────────ဆဝ၄─────────────

Untouchable Passes

Shintaro stared at the ceiling night after night. Tonight was very hot. There was her face, beautiful and far away. His stomach growled.

He threw off the covers, pulled on his clothes. He was out and free. The shudders of the old wooden house that closed off the compartment where he slept were faint behind him. Shintaro looked up into the dark clouds. His chest felt as though it might crack open and fling out his heart. He crossed the tracks and walked on. He would probably never see that pretty white face again, would probably never hear her say those soft, incomprehensible things. Unless by some act of fate he should bump into her on the subway, or in a coffee shop. But what were the chances of that in Tokyo? He visualized the situation. They smiled, said hello. Then what? What did one say to a beautiful woman? What did one say to a woman? To an American one? He pondered these problems until he came to the next street lamp, where he pulled Maximilian's business card out of his wallet.

No one knew better than Maximilian what to say to a beautiful English-speaking woman. But Maximilian was strange. It might not be worth it if Maximilian had to be there, too. Shintaro found himself leaning against the gate to the shrine. He had never seen the grounds of a shrine. Strange for a Japanese, he thought. His mother had said that there was one such shrine outside his home town, but that he and his people had not been allowed to enter it. Now it was a family tradition never to go to the shrine. In the last two towns they had lived in, they had never gone to the shrine. He pushed the gate open. Looked up at the pointed treetops. He would someday pierce the sky like them. He entered the shrine.

He climbed the stairs carved out of the hillside. The path wound around the hill; from one side he could see the station and all the people hurrying home, and from the other side, the rows of plants in the rice fields, and beyond them, his house, asleep with the other houses. He stood on the hilltop before the forbidden shrine and looked down on everything. Felt satisfied, as if he'd made it all himself. He lay down on the steps of the shrine. The wind swept across his face and arms, filled his shirt-sleeves and pant legs with its softness so that he forgot he was wearing clothes. The sky descended onto his small body from all angles. It breathed into his tiny life, never stopping to examine any one thing or another or rooting out incidents to make him wince or regret. Welcome to the shrine, the wind seemed to say as it passed over every mishap until his mistakes were erased and forgotten, and he was purely himself. He breathed deeply. Something seemed to drop away from him and sink down through the stone steps into the ground beneath. He fell asleep.

On the borderland of a dream, Shintaro heard something calling his name, and fell deeper into slumber. It knew his name and had power over his name, so he followed the voice deeper into the forest. One of the symbols in that confusing place was himself, not traveling, but lying still, sleeping, on somebody's doorstep, somebody who did not take to strangers. Everything would be all right if only he could remember the name of the somebody. But no, all he could think as he lay there paralyzed was the fear of the greatness and terribleness of the dweller of the shrine. He held his head in his hands like a broken eggshell. Then all at once he heard in soft oceanic tones that he need only forget his own name to remember the name of the power that lived beyond the doorstep. Then he could pray and be safe. He listened to the creaking of the pines. Opened his eyes to discover that his vision had become total: he could see in every direction at once. He watched the countryside below grow faint as the gold leaf on the shrine glowed brighter and sucked the light from the world, absorbed and guarded the light while the people, safe and ignorant in their dark houses, slept. Shintaro concentrated on forgetting his name. The shrine was light itself. He lay immobile on the shrine steps. He had to forget. It would be too late, would be too dangerous to stay here without knowing the name of . . . of . . . He could not forget his own name, could not remember the name of the Power living in that shrine. Shintaro's name was a precious thing that no one recognized or remembered. Certainly they would not make him forget it. Certainly they could not. He had to leave, but his body would not move. Shintaro watched. The shrine grew brighter. It caught fire and leapt into dazzling flames so tall that they erased the moon from the sky. Tears streamed down his face and wet the steps. The fire dried them. Leapt to his clothes. Burned them off his body. Now he was free. He ran into the touchable world. Thus began the hunt.

The first arrow whizzed past his left ear. The sacrifice flung himself into the underbrush, though he was sure it would be nearly impossible to find his way out again. He tore his way through the branches. They scraped his face and legs. The arrows were coming after him. They teemed like rain around him and crunched under his bare feet. Amidst the fleet was one forbidden golden arrow, which he could not help but pick up. At last, straightening up to run again, the sacrifice heard the shouts of the hunters all around him; he was surrounded. The golden arrow slipped from his hand. An arrow struck him in the arm, not the wooden arrow of a hunter, but a golden arrow of the god himself. His punishment. The untouchable yanked at the arrow and then saw that instead of blood pouring forth from his arm around the golden shaft, a coarse blanket of hair grew out of the wound and covered his skin. His chest and body wherever he looked disappeared beneath this blanket. The arrow broke off. The wound disintegrated. He had been changed into a wild boar.

He had no desire to marvel over this metamorphosis, only to barrel further into the underbrush. The hunters were there in front of him, but as they did not recognize him immediately, he was able to break through their ring. Their hounds bit at his heels. The chase was on. The untouchable doubled back in the direction of the shrine. The hunters shouted. He leapt out of the brush. But instead of arriving once more at the shrine, he had come to the edge of a cliff. Now he was sure that he would never find his way out of this dream place alone. The hunters leapt out of the brush after him. He teetered on the edge of the cliff and fell over the edge, was stuck once again by the god's golden arrow. It changed him into a bird. He tried to fly, but was weighed down by exhaustion. A hundred wooden arrows pierced his feathers. It was then that he knew the name of the deity that had saved him many times. He pronounced the name. The god's eyes flamed and burned the sight out of the sacrifice. The god hung above him like a guardian angel. The boy was not afraid; he did not know who he was or had been. As the blood ran out of his heart, he assumed his human form. The god laid his hands on the boy's body, and breathed these words: "My son, now you must remake me. Let me hide myself within your shape so that people will never know why it is I —" Before he finished his speech, he had leapt into the boy's mouth.

Shintaro stared up into a sheet of blackness. There were no stars. It had begun to rain. He jumped up. Looked around. He could not remember the name of the deity. The wind whistled through the pines. His body was wet and clammy. He was shivering. Where was he? He had never believed in such places. Shintaro pulled his jacket around his shoulders and started down the path. The rhythm of his feet on the steps set his mind wandering to Kabukicho, to Sazzae, to Lois.

Then he realized he had forgotten to make a wish. He turned around. Hurried back up the steps. Fished through his pocket for a ten yen piece. There was the golden grating, and behind it, the altar. His foot touched the top step. He moved cautiously forward, the wish formulating in his thoughts. He tossed the coin in, clasped his hands together, froze mind and body. Something was moving behind the grate. A black figure. Shintaro stared at it. He stared harder. It stopped. Shintaro stepped backward. Lost his balance. Tried to regain it, but only succeeded in grasping the air before toppling down the steps. Mud. Rain. He looked once more into the black sheet of sky. His eyes focused. He picked himself up. There was the grating, the golden altar, and beyond it in a fighting stance, a wooden statue. Shintaro moved closer. Yes, it was just the statue of the painted deity that guarded the shrine. He laughed, but his laughter was hollow. He fell silent, his wish unmade.

Chapter 18

Fighter, Fighter

The scorpion in a ring of fire would wield its tale into its own back rather than be consumed. English teachers and other animals chase their tails around and around.

The street rumbled as the trains passed underneath. Someone's girlfriend stretched to kiss her man, kiss, and was enclosed in the crowd. Day-Glo skirts fluttered into the stairwells, downward-winding, all-extinguishing. At this hour it always seemed that something dark would erupt in the ironwork mazes beneath the city. The midnight sky enclosed Lois. Time was running out. The living had been exiled by the inaudible click of ten thousand tiny golden second hands. To the catacombs!

Yet the scorpion remained, listening to her internal dialogue — chasing her tale — waiting until the body of the earth ignited and revealed her terrible mind. Lo's co-workers had disappeared down another hallway. She forgot to say goodnight. They were all a little tipsy. Maybe they didn't notice. Or maybe it was they who forgot, and she was the one who didn't notice. Would that make her in or out? Maybe it was better staying out. Perhaps there was no inside. Nobody home.

A scream. "Mommy!" a voice screamed. Her unborn daughter?

She looked around, but there was no one. She straightened up. When you heard someone call you like that, it was from another dimension. Who had told her that? Perhaps it was the white queen begging her to resolve the painting. She walked along to Sazzae. The taste of whale lingered in her mouth. Her date had begged her to try it. He was probably telling his friends now that he got an American to eat whale. She wouldn't go out with him again. And she wouldn't tell anyone. Anyway, there was nothing she could do: it was already dead. As dead as the white queen and the song about doomed Maximilian in her painting. Maybe it wasn't really *her* painting. The black shape that was not yet real was fighting for life and eroded the reality on the canvas. It seemed presumptuous to think *she'd* given something reality. Maybe it was a mere repetition of a deeper truth. To have been or not to be, was there any room for question? She was alone on the bridge they had been on that morning.

It occurred to her that reality was to be believed in, like a god. It descended upon circles of worshippers. The faithless could not see it and could only create as far as their lack of vision hazarded. *Content yourself to search out new illusions, to make people see them. That is your work.*

The pale green trains swiveled toward her like fish. They disappeared into the wall beneath her feet. She crossed the street and went down the stairwell. She bought a token and ran down two more flights of stairs, through the corridors, left, right, left, and up the next two flights. Stopped at the top to catch her breath and then pushed her way into the nearest line. The trains looked big and real down here, surreal. She listened to her inspiration.

The white lady told her to make illusion painful reality. *Aspire to reality.*

But what if it wasn't meant to be her?

Says who? You slip through ten thousand loops only to bind yourselves most inextricably. You who laugh and breathe and bleed too loud, who walk and talk and think too loud.

Sazzae's neon sign cut through the night. The wooden door of the club opened and shut. Inside, the student-, captive-, master-, spirit-hearted folk cackled and drank their brew swaying and standing, dancing, hugging, licking, biting, frothing at the mouths. Each time the door opened, it let out a *wah, wah.* A communal voice that emitted a primal, *wah, wah,* and each time the door shut, it let out no sound at all and, in fact, was camouflaged and ceased to be a door. The owner wafted about exchanging full glasses for empty ones. *Wah,* the wooden door opened again. She chased her tail into the room.

Her ears adjusted to the communal scream. Her eyes adjusted to the darkness. Everyone was back, as if they'd never left. No, they'd never left. No one ever left. They went on this way. She closed the door. It folded into its shadow and was gone. Poof. The room's darkness became intelligible. Her eyes glossed over Caucasian, olive, and black sweating skin. She breathed deeper. Men, she thought. There's one in every city. How nice it'd be to have a man, not a boy. She'd had more than enough boys. You looked at them starry-eyed once or twice, and they were all aflame. Then you walked all over them like hot coals. No. There was too much guilt involved in that transaction. It wasn't worth it anymore. Now a man, a man could last forever, she thought, although for all her vast experience, she had never come into contact with one. Yes, she thought, she needed a man to keep her in line. A man as dangerous as herself, to take her on. She needed a man with an edge.

On the other side of the room all aglow in the spotlight of her eyes stood Maximilian, divine hand gripping a fluorescent drink. Maximilian's perpetual eyes canvassed the room, not resting on any one thing. The hard part would be getting the boy to overcome his shyness. Maximilian didn't talk to anyone. This particular plan required a great deal of subtlety and patience as could be measured by the rapidly expanding space opening in the crowd around him. No one approached him. He was in one of his meditative moods and could make people look ridiculous with little effort. It came in handy when bosses tried to get on his case, and when he was working out a plan like this one. Flattery was the key. It could take months of praising the boy's male beauty like no woman could ever do until he was transformed into a dreamy Narcissus. Months he had. The boy would come to see himself as the ideal of beauty based on the aesthetic Maximilian proposed.

He has to be made to see it my way, Maximilian thought. I don't want to pressure him into doing anything he'll regret later. Once Shintaro becomes an idol, he'll be free. Maximilian chugged his gin-and-tonic. The boy was so shy, it could take years. The wooden door opened, *Wha, wha,* and shut again. Maximilian and everyone else in the room looked up.

Shintaro. A historic night in the annals of Sazzae.

Maximilian looked quickly away and immediately saw that the others were dumbfounded by Shintaro's beauty. Tonight would be the deciding night. Let's see, lesson number one. He'd let the boy flounder for a while.

Masami the owner ordered them another round of drinks. Maximilian took the drink and praised Masami's new look. Masami's white satin arm wound itself around Maximilian's shoulders. "Jacku dahhhlink, where is my money? The money?" In one fell flash of his black smile Masami destroyed the effect of his angelic white robe.

"I have it. Wait till morning. There are too many people around," Maximilian said, "Come on, get away from me." Masami turned his back. Maximilian reached over the waiter's shoulder and removed a drink from the tray, as well as the plastic glow-in-the-dark halo on Masami's black head. He took a sip of his gin-and-tonic and looked for his shy teen idol. There, pressed against the wall, looking American in his jeans and boots. He'll be fine.

Shintaro was at the height of his capacity for boldness and managed to stare quite audaciously at Lois's dark curly head tilted so gracefully forward, eyes up like a kitten's and emanating that painfully beautiful sense of melancholy. He'd known it. She had to come.

Now she was here. There. Lois, more beautiful than he'd remembered her. Than he'd dreamed her. He could see her violet irises. There was no way to communicate with the dream creature. She spoke dream-language. If only she could hear him sing! Not that it would make a bit of difference. He was not worthy of her. She was *too* beautiful. She belonged to another world. He could never make her love him. And if he could make her love him . . . how could he be so selfish as to defile her? And if he could be so selfish as to defile her, how long could he hide from her? To think of ruining such a creature, he must be abominable, not even human. No. She would find out. And what then? What would be left of him if the most precious thing in his life refused him, thought he was dirty and refused to touch him?

By now, the three had exiled themselves to the three walls where the bar was not, to wait with their reputations at stake. Three doubts. Nerves exposed to the air. Each grew still as a jungle cat waiting for nothing, never, slowly.

A man with an edge wouldn't let you burn him out. No, he'd trash your whole life first. Your family's. Your hometown's. Your friends'.

A long time and a lot of subtlety. Patience. Work. That was the way it would have to be; the kid could never become a teen idol by himself.

How long before she found out, before she called him dirty? Untouchable? How long?

Not entirely aware of being watched, they stared into space, into the chasm between them at *Savoir-Faire*, the exaggerated postures, the sublime haggling arabesques of heavily perfumed, leather dolls.

An edge. Yea. Friday-night-nothing at Survivor.

Shy idol. Boys-will-be-boys, lipstick as red as the walls.

How long?

The smoke, the music, the beat, beat, American beat, Sazzae. No. Not American, not Japanese, neither cure nor escape, not anything. And the *rhythmica intoxica* went on. Every head swam to the thud. Drinks drowned out those time cards, those trains, everybody enclosed now in the purply walls of the throb. Everybody feeding off the same Fliday-night-slazzae.

Running on empty and running fast, one found oneself on the verge of making treacherous leaps of faith. Especially standing against a wall peering into one chasm at your front if only to avoid the nausea of the other Friday-night-nothing off to the side, rocking on the beat, waiting not for nothing. Hanging, in fact, already hanging by one finger over a ravine so deathly deep, so steep and full of stalagmites that one has either to pull oneself back to safety, or fly.

Climbing back to safety, Maximilian was bound to meet himself, face-to-face, weapon in hand. But then flying, he would surely move the market, and compel innocent followers to their depths. For, the only thing more alluring than a flyer flying briefly before awakening torn and tattered at the foot of someone else's cliff is the impossibility of making it to the other side.

Chapter 19

―――――――――――‿‿‿――――――――――――

Someone Else's Cliff

Another moment's hesitation would have etched their young figures in purgatory — it was in the rules — when suddenly, a wallet dropped on the dance floor. No one saw it, except Maximilian, who was wont to notice such things. And Lo, who noticed the things that Maximilian was noticing. All three looked around the room to see if anyone else was noticing the event, and discovered each other being watched and watching each other: *Oh.*

Maximilian leaned back, one leg bent against the wall, sipped his drink. Lo and Shintaro pretended to look away. They watched Maximilian out of the corners of their eyes, watched him pushing himself away from the wall, conversing his way over to the dance floor, then staring silently into space. Now he was the only one in the room emitting a great silence. All the while, he feigned distraction, posed. Lo watched intently. It was all too smooth, as if it had been rehearsed a thousand times before. For a split second, Maximilian looked as if he owned the wallet. And then it was over; he had it. Lo looked around the room. No one noticed except Shintaro, whose name she had forgotten, whose almond eyes were widening, looking at Lo.

Maximilian had disappeared from the dance floor. Out of nowhere, Masami's voice bloomed in her ear. Hissed, "Don't bother with Jack." She scratched her ear and kept looking around the dance floor, but Maximilian wasn't anywhere to be seen. "He's a womanizer," the voice said.

"Oh yeah? I'd knock horns with Maximilian, any day," she said. She turned toward Masami. He glared at her. Lo pushed off from her wall, went to the dance floor.

There she was. So beautiful! Shintaro pushed off from his wall, wandered to the edge of the dance floor.

Maximilian's stomach tied itself into a knot.

Where did he go? Lo turned around, stood face-to-face with Shintaro. "Where's Maximilian?" she said.

"Who?"

Maximilian was weaving his way through the crowd to the bar. He ordered three gin-and-tonics. They appeared immediately. "Hello," Maximilian said. He smiled. All three smiled and tried not to look at each other. Now adept at pushing silences to their limits, they let this one go on. It was like a game, competing to see who was the best at telepathy *à la japonais*. Having figured out what the Japanese meant by sitting together without talking with words, the problem for Maximilian and Lo was how to relax amidst an imposing silence. Surely it was a question of listening. The mood shifted. They breathed through a dialogue of raw presence. Maximilian looked at Lo. At last Shintaro took it upon himself to find the appropriate words: "Uh." Now the boy was pulling a small dictionary out of his pocket, flipping through it. "Uh," he said again, "It tastes like lime."

"I like people who can't speak English." Maximilian said, "They have to rely one hundred percent on their sense of humor. Enjoy that drink," he said to Shintaro. "You're only getting one."

"O.K.," the boy said. "I think so." His face became very serious.

"Don't worry; this time I'll take better care of you."

"Thank you."

"No problem."

Lo wondered if Maximilian planned to take better care of her, too. She swilled her way to the bottom of her glass. There was another gin-and-tonic in her hand in no time. "Thanks," she said.

A table emptied, and they slid into the seats, their three worlds sublimated, contracting into a recognizable social unit. The regular fungi turned around to look at them at their table. They bore themselves like subterranean plants. Maximilian took control, not soliciting their conversation. He would be civilized to the extent that he was not forced to socialize. Shintaro took out a pen. Lo watched him open his dictionary. He seemed to be composing. He folded the piece of paper and handed it to her. Maximilian froze on the edge of his seat, heard her ask. "What is it?" He watched her unfold it. He leaned forward, and they read it together. In Shintaro's neat square handwriting was written:

To a sleepless moon
Through window shudder walks
My late-night haiku.

She flipped the paper over, and over, wrote,

He drinks neither sun nor air
But scoffs and says he is best,
Whose world is impotent,
And holds no joy.

She folded the paper. Shintaro pretended not to see, as she handed the paper to Maximilian, who nudged Shintaro and handed the paper back.

"I'm going to see about the package that you said you would deliver," Maximilian said, "and that never arrived."

"Did I say that? I will deliver it."

"It was urgent."

"Next time say so."

Maximilian found Masami skulking behind the bar. Masami had changed his clothes. He parted his blond wig to argue with Maximilian about money. Shintaro was deciphering the poem with his dictionary.

"You cannot understand your Maximilian," Masami said to Lois.

"The weak will survive and the strong will live," Maximilian said.

"Our Maximilian is a rebel, a savage," said Masami, rattling his bracelets.

"You have no manners," she said.

"Can you cook?" Maximilian's conceit was enough to awe her ignorance.

"What?" she said.

"You're all right."

"All right? That's watery."

He laughed. "I feel like I can do anything."

"Well you can't."

"Yes I can. Watch." He stretched and yawned.

Lois stole one of his cigarettes. She saw him see her stealing one of his cigarettes, *caught*, and she said, "Why don't you buy your own cigarettes?"

"Who's who here? Men are supposed to project." He grabbed his cigarettes.

"Don't proselytize," said Lo.

Masami massaged Maximilian's shoulders. "Prostitute is more like it," said Masami.

Maximilian leaned toward Lo and lit the projectionist's cigarette. He said thank you for her.

"As we cannot presume to understand the forces of the universe in any way other than human, it is self-deceptive to refuse giving personalities to the creator and the destroyer, and everyone in between. You never know who you're talking to," said Lo. "It could be gods."

"I'm trying to be inspiring. Sickness inspires art."

"A healthy society would be art itself. With no ugliness, man would feel no need to communicate his vision of beauty."

"Don't vote for her," said Maximilian to Shintaro.

"Don't you have enough natural limitations without constructing imaginary ones?" Lo said.

Maximilian considered her. "I face an obstacle, I make it look easy. If you don't see achievement in ease, you're jealous. Like my Tiki fish stock tip. Anyone can buy it, but most people don't believe in making money the easy way."

"Is *that* where your money comes from?" Masami crooned. "I want some of that." Maximilian launched into his hard sell for Tiki fish. Masami was ready to borrow from friends and acquaintances to buy enough of the fish stock.

"Do you believe in God?" Lois asked.

"Can't you tell by my halo?" Maximilian looked at Masami, whose smile switched on.

"You're so touchy," said Masami. "Isn't he?" he said to Shintaro, and repeated the question in Japanese.

"I don't know," said Shintaro.

"Misfits," Masami said, and went to turn up the music. Shintaro pocketed his dictionary.

"Through thievery the aristocrat becomes almost human," Lois observed.

"But you'll deliver that info tomorrow?" Maximilian asked.

"Today," Lois said.

Maximilian inched over to Masami who was asking for help moving the center table out of the way of the dancers. The table was heavy, but the two men's faces remained expressionless. It was a ritual with them. At this point in the evening they carried the table like two figurines in a bell tower, the owner looking out for where they were going, Maximilian following, both bending, straightening, stiffly walking, bending to put the table down, then quitting each other without a glance.

The owner cranked up the music. Shintaro stood awkwardly on the fringes of the expanded dance floor with no one to talk to. Lo was lost in the music. Shintaro clung to his full glass. Adrift. And then Maximilian's voice was in his ear. "I've been looking for a friend like you for years. You are the statue I have seen in my dreams."

Shintaro stared straight ahead at Lo. She had worked herself into a tight swing on the dance floor. Double time, half time, on time, her feet not moving very much at all, her face turned up to the ceiling, eyes closed. Her hair swiveled in back as she worked the floor and the tensions of her limbs which were winding this way and that like rubber bands pulling always into her center. She seemed to be doing all this absentmindedly. Other people watched her, too. Shintaro shifted his attention to these others. They watched and then imitated her movements. One by one they filled the floor. They pushed her to the center of the dance, revolved around her shimmery hair, her floating feet. They were trying to dance with her, but she only danced back at one of them.

Shintaro's eyes widened. He arched his neck to get a better look at the man dancing in front of Lo. He had a cummerbund at his waist, and a Spencer jacket. His short pants were cuffed above his hoofs. Shintaro tried to get a better look at the goat's hoofs dancing in front of Lo. Smoke obliterated the center of the dance floor. There seemed to be a breeze in the room. Maximilian returned, stood next to Shintaro, followed the boy's eyes to the center of the dance floor. "She's not such a bad girl."

"What?" Shintaro said.

"Not bad."

Shintaro looked into Maximilian's blue eyes.

"O.K., she's a good dancer."

"Yes," Shintaro said.

"The macho woman is not only aware of her sexuality . . . . Do you want to dance?"

"Oh, no. I can't dancing."

"Can't dance! But you want to be a singer, right?"

"Right, but . . . I can't dancing, because of my shy," he said.

Maximilian assumed an unusually serious tone. "Your shy is not to be protected. A singer cannot be shy."

"I know, but . . ." Shintaro turned away a little, vainly hoping that Maximilian would sympathize and change the subject. Didn't he know that shyness was a good quality in Japan?

"Well, what will you be if you cannot become a singer?"

Shintaro started. The blue eyes pierced his defenses. "I don't know," he said, "I . . . I will become a singer."

"So you want to be less shy?"

"What?"

"Um . . . do you want to 'lose your shy'?"

"Yes, but —"

"You're not aware that you are the most beautiful boy I'll ever meet, are you? Your forehead, your nose are perfection. They don't even belong to you. They're timeless, everyone's." Shintaro was not used to having a friend. He wasn't sure he understood Maximilian's words but began to see himself in the mirror of

113

Maximilian's eyes, saw his own forehead, his own lovely nose, and like Narcissus, turned his face to meet the beautiful lips that he'd dreamed up. A kiss descended on him from the mirror. He felt himself swimming through another body. All eyes were on them as Shintaro separated from Maximilian. "Let's dance," the mirror said.

Shintaro gazed into the vibrating bodies. There she was, always disappearing, re-appearing, smiling, then cool, distracted, and laughing with her half-breed partner. Shintaro's shoulders tightened. If he had learned to dance a long time ago, he'd be able to save her.

"You don't know how attractive you are, do you, Shintaro? Have you seen how people light up when you come near them? No woman could resist you, and dancing increases your beauty," Maximilian said.

Shintaro's face became desperate. "No. I can't dancing.

"I'll teach you everything."

Shintaro's eyes hadn't moved from Lo's shoulders.

"I know people who can help you audition at the record company. But they don't accept shy singers."

Shintaro stared blankly ahead.

"O.K., forget it. I can't teach you to dance. Dancers dance because they're listening to something in them that's always listening to the music and always wanting to dance, and if you don't have that thing, you can't play, and you can't dance."

Shintaro watched her sweating face, smooth, untroubled as if lost in a dangerous sleep. Her hair tumbled down, swung to the right, swung to the left, backlashed up. She seemed to have found her way into a new body, a tangling body of human pillars that was holding the ceiling apart from the floor. He had to save her. "I got it," Shintaro said into Maximilian's blue eyes.

"You did?"

"Yes. I see."

Maximilian smiled into his glass.

Shintaro swallowed half of his gin-and-tonic at once and set the glass down on one of the tables. He took a deep breath and turned to Maximilian.

"O. K., now first, listen to the music. Don't think, just feel the beat."

"The beat?"

"Yes. The rhythm." Maximilian beat his palm against his knee.

"Oh. The beat?"

"Yes." Maximilian held both of Shintaro's forearms, and made the boy hold his. Shintaro closed his eyes, and Maximilian began pushing him from side to side with every other beat. Once Shintaro caught on, Maximilian sped up and hit every beat. "Good," he said. It was true. Shintaro had good rhythm. Maximilian continued pushing him back and forth.

A bead of sweat rolled down from Shintaro's forehead and hung on his cheek like a tear. He didn't open his eyes.

Maximilian started to let go of the boy's arms. He should be able to do it on his own now. But Shintaro's hands fell limply down to his sides. His eyes opened, and he stopped.

Maximilian laughed and grabbed the boy's bronze wrists.

When Shintaro opened his eyes the second time, he found they had drifted into the center of the floor and were dancing next to Lois. He mustn't stop. He twisted his hands free and struggled to keep the beat. Now the music seemed to make perfect sense. He was a machine. The thrill of it threw him off balance as the song ended.

"That was really good!" Maximilian said.

"It was difficult."

Lois was at his side. "Do you like this music, Shintaro?"

"The music get louder when I dance."

ROUND III

Chapter 20

───────ಲ⦿ಲ───────

Trio

It must have been the metallic quality in the air that heightened their perceptions that September. They were young, and although the leaves had turned red, they were not in school. Or perhaps it was this latest crop of Japanese youth abandoning work ethics mid-stream, here, at the pinnacle of their heritage finally coming of age on the scene. On the verge of rotting on the vine, too ripe for foreign examples to show them how to procure the rites of the leisure crass.

Their work ethic relaxed, although, they hadn't met again. Maximilian's options account was up over two million. He was especially proud of those puts he'd sold, and bought 100 more call options on Tiki fish. He left off trying to calculate his bonus and walked with a spring in his step. Shintaro didn't answer Maximilian's calls, so Maximilian stopped answering his phone, until one day when there was a lull in the markets, waiting for nothing, the September unemployment number, he picked up the phone. It was Lois. There was no way to do it without her, no point in waiting any longer.

The threesome eased into familiarity, meeting here and there. Their eyes met in the various establishments of the *gaijin* ghetto, Roppongi. And after Shintaro got the convocation letter for the record company audition, Maximilian insisted as a matter of pride that Lois get in free posing as a model, which didn't seem too far-fetched since most of the western clientele either modeled or spent a lot of money and attracted chic Japanese customers. The three glamour clubbers struck poses of egotistical disbelief getting ready for Shintaro's future role as a teen idol, and theirs as his entourage. Concentrating on the public, they barely noticed the threat to their private selves and ignored the pain in their laughter. The harsh Tokyoscape was no kick in *their* eye. The trio wandered the streets of Roppongi. Could this glee go on?

In October, there was another party. Only Lois was interesting to Shintaro, but there were voices and faces to deal with. Suddenly they were in the middle of things. It was metallic. It was the magnetism of Maximilian, most of them supposed, Jack of all trades, who by some trick of the air managed to cultivate a scene between the expatriate cracks of Tokyo this night, that fall. He was the only one who understood the economics of spiritualism and had the foresight to afford an apartment big enough to hold them. A spontaneous combustion took place. The anti-structure opened a new world of possibilities.

Climbing the stairs to Maximilian's apartment, they

could taste the sky. The door was wide open for any who cared to enter the bare carpeted rooms. They nodded without saying a word, and checked out the unknowns through the corners of their eyes. Taking off their shoes or lighting their cigarettes was bliss, for nothing had happened yet. They were in form and self-reliant.

A dozen people had already found their way up to Maximilian's apartment by the time Maximilian himself arrived home. A girl and a boy were talking in the corner. They slipped in and out of their mutual accents, a Morse code of mother tongues. The images kept everything going; they sat on the floor and reconstructed their ideals in a repetition of youth. Wherever there were adept followers, there was someone to assume the patchwork of fantasies, stretch the illusory cloth to fit a naked persona. Maximilian did not seem to notice them. He walked straight into his living room without taking off his shoes, turned on his answering machine, and wrote down the messages. Then he looked at their waiting faces and rolled his eyes.

Real followers were hard to come by since any lack was attributable to them. When they were weak, they were just a group of people with nebulous ideals. Then they flexed their social muscle. The enormous effort on their part to keep Maximilian symbolically intact risked erupting into 'the new morality', as Shintaro called it.

Maximilian took advantage of his position farthest from the doorway to lean back into the shadow of a screen. Lois, next to him, had dropped two ice cubes into a glass of gin.

"Thank you my dear," Maximilian said, and put on

some jazz. A girl named Sachiko got up to open the window. Someone found a real ashtray. Lo and Sachiko changed places, feigned relaxation. They were alive. Lois tore her attention away from a Japanese conversation she knew was about her to Maximilian and Shintaro, who were finally talking in what seemed to her to be unusually friendly tones. They'd made some kind of agreement, maybe regarding Shintaro's audition. She couldn't quite figure it out, but they were bonding and made it clear that she had no role. Here they were all three together in the same room, and Maximilian was laughing, calling for a toast, "To Shintaro, who is going to land his first record contract, as a teen idol. 'To Tomorrow'!" They clinked glasses. Bottoms up. The stereo blared new music Maximilian must have had sent from the States. "Record contract? 'Tomorrow'?" people asked. Shintaro didn't know what to do and denied any such intention.

"What record contract?" Two Europeans looked up from their discussion of Vienna to get a glimpse of the next teen idol. Then they went back to the 1860s.

Lo couldn't help listening to their conversation. Could they have said 'Maximilian'? My Maximilian? It seemed the Emperor of Mexico was from Vienna. "Is that right?" she asked.

"Yes, Maximilian was his name."

Sachiko knelt down to turn up the volume. She twisted to her feet in her leather mini skirt. Her hair was pulled into a proud ponytail that swished from side to side as her body moved to the music. A couple of people stopped talking, eyes on Satchiko in her hot pink lipstick. She began to dance. She focused on the floor, on the ceiling, never on anyone's face. One of the Vienna boys said, "Pretty." His friend agreed. Maximilian paced about at the front door on the telephone. He was ordering sushi for Shintaro.

Lois was hungry, too. Was that a consideration? They were pretending they knew something she didn't. She knew she loved Maximilian because he wasn't available. Because she never knew where she stood with him. When she whispered, he was too far away to hear. When she catapulted insults, he was already at her side. There was nothing she could be sure of, whether she was in or out. There was the white queen, and she was definitively inside, no matter how hard Lois had tried to push her out. But if that mythical creature could shape her canvas, why not the scene in front of her? Maximilian was from Vienna.

Lois had wandered into the library. She opened the bay window, and sat on the floor looking out at the October night. When she leaned out, she could see the party through the window next to her. The neighbors would surely complain. She saw Maximilian put down the telephone. People were trying to involve him in the party, but he deflected their attempts.

Maximilian seized Shintaro's arm. "How are your singing lessons coming?"

"The teacher doesn't have a nice voice, but her English pronunciation is good. I will take Lois' English conversation class."

"I have something you'll like," Maximilian said. He pulled a new CD from the shelf and ripped off the plastic. "Come in here."

Shintaro followed him into the dark library.

Maximilian put the CD on. He closed the door. Shintaro's body stiffened. Maximilian was reaching for the light switch. A draft carried the sound of laughter in through the open window. They felt her presence in the room. Shintaro leaned back against the door. She was with them in the library. The neon light from the sign outside cast its red light on her. They listened to the musician lay bare truth on the frontier of the electric violin. A landscape where they could only listen.

When he saw Lois by the window, Maximilian withdrew his hand from the light switch. There was no need to turn on the light. He stood straight in the dark holding the CD case. Lois watched Maximilian, statuesque, larger than life. Shintaro saw her hidden in the window seat on the mat floor. A little girl listening to the violin solo. She memorized the moment so that they could be here together, all three of them, forever. The violin was sad and low, like a funeral. She made a mental halt, as if checking things at the door. Which part of them would continue? Proceed how? Lois looked at her two friends.

She would change the picture. A ballerina danced on the insides of her eyelids. The will to dance had usurped all minor subjects, had displaced their conversation with floating arabesques that carried with them an obligation, since she, having conceived of them, was the only one to carry them out. A rain dance. She would make it rain. She stood up, shook her limbs. In motion, *ça va*. She closed her eyes and was for a higher cause. With friends. Lois ballerina, a floating thing unwrapping imaginary veils, uncoiling free and skinless, uncoiling down to nothing.

They watched. Red neon light was enough as they listened to the violinist lay bare the truth in a detached voice. A thread. How could they proceed in this family that they had become?

On the frontier of the truth, the atonal violin sang taboo, and there was no way out. We think love in movies is true, our own puny loves, tired imitations with no background music, so I only mention her here as a tool, a scalpel, hammer, mirror — she changed life and law, unearthed, the plow tilling the land. No means to break her, of the race of time, as she spilled through my fingers. A creative force, a solution lying from within the problem. It was beside the point that she was beautiful. We avoided confrontation, and continued to expect. She was change and immediacy. Most multi-generation simulcasts refuse to live in the past, present and future, and deny existence itself. No incarnation. No cycle beginning with the consummation of a neither naturally nor societally taboo act.

"Let's get married," Lois whispered.

Maximilian stood straight in the dark, holding the CD case. Shintaro barely breathed. All three listened to the sad, low, violin as if at a funeral.

Denial settled in after a series of chain reactions. Repetition of consequences. Through successive lives, the lovers grew apart in unwilling catharsis. Guilty permutations that worked through their lives. Oh cyclical drama.

They turned to each other, naked, except for their clothes, were neither male nor female, just the tension that defined them, a beam, dynamic tension, the river who he would like her to become, opposites.

"Is she taking off her clothes?" A man in the other room said through the open window. The smell of autumn came in. Lois danced with her eyes closed. She was a flower.

"Why not? She's such a slut."

The music reverted to a medieval order, heavy as old perfume — Lois might as well have been wearing a red velvet Elizabethan dress supporting her naked breasts — until the violin changed to another truth, and then another, as she flashed before them, a myriad of sexual personae. Taboo assumed the form of music at the beach in ancient swimwear, carnival in feathers and sequins. A slow march in riding costume. Something to remember with the flash of a camera. In a pill-box hat and elbow-length gloves. Her suitors' lenses turned, diaphragm opened. With aprons, smiling, despite the rubber gloves. All thighs in high-heel pumps. She met herself coming and going with the violinist's dynamic imposition. Despite him, she met herself, in the mirror, with a hammer, with a scalpel.

"I've seen her somewhere before," came through the window.

Chapter 21

―――――――――ℰℭ―――――――――

Blind Potential

At Sazzae, Maximilian announced that he was going to New York.

"You mean I'm stuck here in Tokyo, and you're going to America?" Lois asked. "Just like that?"

"Yeah."

"Oh."

"Can you watch my apartment?"

"What about *my* apartment?"

"I'm going to be traveling a lot from now on. All you have to do is answer the phone."

"Will *you* call?" She looked at her hands. Maximilian was so mysterious. She remembered her friend's underworld spy letter.

But Maximilian liked his freedom. "Hm. Then again you're dangerous."

"You're dangerous: you're a coward."

"All you have to do is answer the phone." He towered over her. "Break your lease."

Moving day came. Shintaro lay in bed with a fever, although they hadn't told him about it. Maximilian hired some movers. She took one last look out her window at the building fifteen feet away with its wife beatings and love makings. Lois barely lifted a finger. She and Maximilian rode behind the moving van. Her paintings rode on top. Maximilian arrived at a stoplight as if descending on a target. She remembered her ex-roommate's letter, which had arrived after Maximilian had come back from the United States. They said they heard she was sleeping with the underworld spy.

Hardly. What underworld spy? She glanced at him in the drivers' seat next to her. It fit like a shadow. He was so secretive. She would observe his shadow while he was gone, she thought. She was moving in. Now she would be like family, only he wasn't telling the truth. She sensed the danger. This time, she would notice things she'd passed over on other visits. Like the mail for another person that came to his apartment because, he said, the former tenant hadn't changed his address at the post office. "It's most generous of you to let me stay in your apartment rent-free," she said.

"Sometimes more is less," he said. "It's hard to find someone decent to house-sit. After a certain point, friends become thieves. They steal what's already theirs. Just don't ransack the place."

"You already bought me for nothing at a garage sale. I think no ransacking is asking a bit too much."

"Can I make a U-turn here?"

"I'm just kidding. I'll be nice."

"That's nice to hear. I've got my convictions, too. Or at least I will as soon as I raise enough money. You have to pick your battles. No point in rushing in like cannon fodder."

"Rushing in where?"

"I don't know yet. I'm enjoying blind potential."

The haphazard Tokyoscape rattled past her window. Maybe he had a good reason for secrecy. Americans were innocent until proven guilty. Still, she felt she was in danger. Maybe not directly in danger. Maybe it was someone in her family, or someone so close to her that she felt the danger herself, like a severed limb. Was he that close to her? She didn't even know his last name. Maybe this was not going to work. They carried her boxes up the stairs. He unlocked the door onto his sprawling appointments. He set her box down on the floor in front of her rooms. She could see into his bedroom to an oak desk with a single jealous drawer.

He was standing behind her. "Do you come with an instruction manual?"

She blushed and sat down on the couch. "Did you just say that to get a reaction?"

"Slowly. That's too sophisticated for me."

"No doubt," she said.

He looked stung. She felt sorry for not giving him a way out. She could see how he might be insulted by her cross-examination if he really weren't hiding anything. "I'm easy to live with," she said. "You just have to compensate for my second-guessing."

"You know," he said, "I'm not really good at analysis. I've never said this before, so it's good we're talking about it, but my mind lags behind my body."

"You do have a nice body," she said.

"No, I'm serious. I've always known that my mind was a little bit slower than my body. And now that I'm getting older, I'm a little bit worried because I don't have my mind to fall back on. That's where you come in. In twenty years, people who have it the other way around will be at an advantage because they'll be able to concentrate on mental things."

Was he playing a game? "You will be a stunningly debonair fifty-year-old, and I hope I'm there to see you. Anyway, I don't think your body is ahead of your mind."

"Either I take that as a compliment to my mind or an insult to my body."

"You are wise," she lied. "That's an analytical faculty."

"Well, let's take painting. I look at an abstract painting, and I don't understand it. You're supposed to have some kind of feeling, but I don't get anything out of it."

"Think about your impressions. Everybody sees it their own way. Maybe the biggest understanding comes when you look at nature or reality and start to see the abstractions in the world around you."

He parallel parked as if landing a plane, moving the car two centimeters with ease. She had never realized how physically fit he was. What an all-American, corn-dog. He looked at her blankly with his gorgeous blue eyes. She wondered where he'd learned to act. Maybe he was in danger. He'd spoken to her on an emotional level, and touched her deeply. He was her friend. If it was he who was in danger, he was the only one with enough facts to figure out a strategy. She changed her strategy. She would tell him the facts. She would show him her Harvard friend's underworld spy letter. The problem with Harvard friends was that you got off on tangents, and it was hard to get back to reality, although, if the story had gotten back to her, it probably had also been leaked to any miscreant organizations afoot. This line of reasoning had the curious effect of calming her. The ball was out of her court, and Maximilian was strong.

Strong and in danger. Had he put her in danger? She was miffed, unpacking her clothes. Even if he had good cause for not telling her who he really was, he didn't have to screw up her scene in Boston by bragging about sleeping with her. They went out for some butterscotch ice cream, which he chose. It was delicious. He was always hungry. He was delicious. At night, he called down for Italian food. He said, "I better change my name on the door," and went out.

She'd missed her chance to look at the old nameplate. It was already gone like a missing link. "We'll talk about you in the third person," she said as he carried his suitcase out the door.

Chapter 22

~~~~~~

Two

The door to his room remained locked. She unpacked her boxes and let life fall into place. She and Shintaro had stopped going to the clubs and discovered unexpected reserves of energy. He wrote songs and she painted copies of the same painting. Shintaro's grandfather had withdrawn to his laboratory. Shintaro practiced singing American songs for the audition. In the evenings, he took Lois' conversation classes to perfect his pronunciation.

Lois moved her paints out onto Maximilian's terrace. She painted the same subject three different ways. Maximilian, Archduke of Austria on day five as Emperor of Mexico, day six . . . Maximilian's terrace was much more picturesque than hers. Still, one did not move into a man's apartment for the view. One considered whether one belonged there. She roamed the spacious rooms thinking in the long-term and itching to open the drawers and cupboards.

Finally one day, Shintaro was feeling better and,

expecting to find Maximilian, knocked at the door. Lois padded across the living room floor rationalizing, one did not move in for the trappings. One did not abuse one's privileges, but two . . . two might lounge indefinitely in the luxurious apartment on embassy row. Two might thaw out those crab legs, and watch Maximilian's videos as the afternoon wore on. She opened the door: Shintaro.

He stood there in shock. "Is Maximilian here?"

"No. He went away for a while. I'm staying here now."

Shintaro exhaled, relieved. His eyes seized hers. It couldn't be. He was ready to fight it again with every fiber of his body. But looking into her eyes, he fancied the invitation he had been longing for. He had waited so long. He pushed the door open and stepped inside. She looked startled, but said nothing. He felt her breath on his face and gave up fighting. Now he would not let her change her mind. He bent his head close and kissed her lips. Her arms slid up around his neck; her hair fell back across his hands. How long had he wanted this but denied her power, even refused to think of her as a woman? He pressed his body against hers. How could they have raised him to think of this as a profanation?

He watched her pull away and wipe her mouth on her sleeve. She had not invited his kiss after all! His expression transformed from pleasure into so much pain that she reached for his hand reflexively. He enfolded her in his arms again, her skin under his hands. They fell back against the wall. He felt her as separate, and burned to make her part of him. Her breasts, her tummy, her buttocks. She was made for him. Did he carry her? He did not know how they got to the bedroom. She was a tall woman, but in bed she fit his body perfectly. Nor did he know what he did or why he did it as he slid into the folds and crevices. He felt her body open to him like a flower. He gazed down with eyes full of tears at her face and watched her mouth as her lips parted in pleasure. His soul reeled. He clenched her shoulders and gave himself over to maddening desire.

Every muscle in his body relaxed. He was just a man. A man.

They awoke in each other's arms. There was so much of her. He never wanted to let her go. He clung to her as if he were drowning. She watched him kiss her cheeks and forehead as he separated her legs again, and let him repeat his lovemaking.

"Are you hungry?" he said.

"That wasn't hunger? I will cook you some crab legs."

"I'll help you." He followed her into the kitchen.

Shintaro cracked the last crustacean.

Lois emptied the ashtray and opened the window. He followed her. "Let's go out," she suggested, with a sudden sense of urgency, their necks intertwined.

And then they were out. Shintaro was like a river. He rippled as he walked. They went down Aoyamadori to Harajuku. It was Sunday, so the street had been blocked off, and all kinds of food stands erected. The whole street smelled like burning meat. Bicyclers pedaled up and down under the trees. Children got balloons and ice cream, and the teenagers stood around outside Vivre Department Store where a wall of TV screens displayed small pictures of the same thing in varying shades of red, changing to yellow, changing to blue. Pop music blasted into the breezy November afternoon. They passed a teen idol memorabilia stand. "Your face will be on one of these baseball cards," Lois said. She held up a baseball card of a rather homely girl whose teeth were slightly rotting.

"Yuck," Shintaro said.

"She's beautiful!" Lois said.

"I know a much more beautiful woman."

They wandered on past the flea market and the train station. At the end of the street, they could see all the bikers revving up their motorcycles in their leather jackets with 50s teen dolls in frilly skirts, high heels and bathing suits, dancing badly to new-wave music. The two wandered on. Soon everything got a lot quieter. They paused at the entrance to the park. "Did you ever see this shrine?" Shintaro asked.

"No. What shrine?"

"You live in Minato-ku, and you never saw Meiji Jingu Shrine?"

"This is the first time I've ventured out of Maximilian's apartment, except to go to work."

"O.K. Come on."

Their feet crunched down the gravel path. They sounded like horses. Lois broke into a gallop. Shintaro laughed. She faded into the distance. He watched her walking fifty feet ahead, her face turning from the pines on her right, to the clear sky, to the inscription on the flat rock at her left. He didn't bother trying to catch up. He preferred strolling along behind, watching her marvel at everything. Lois turned onto another gravel path with a huge red gate at the end of it, which she, looking at a big black bird in the garden beyond the trees, hadn't noticed yet. Shintaro padded along behind, waiting for her to look up at the gate.

"Wow!" she said at last.

"That's a tori," said Shintaro. "It's the gate to the shrine."

The tori's two vertical posts measured a yard in diameter. Lois walked between these. She looked up at the post connecting them on top and tried to stretch her arms around the post on the left.

Americans were like children. "You can't do it," Shintaro said. He had caught up.

They lowered their voices as they passed under the gates and entered the large gravel yard. Rice-papered buildings surrounded them and the grounds. Off to the left stood Meiji shrine, a low building with wide steps and two huge statues of demons with masses of protruding muscles, hungry jaws and flaming eyes. Shintaro handed Lois a ten yen coin. She watched him bow his head, close his eyes, and a moment later, toss the coin into the wooden box in front of the altar. She did the same. They pressed their noses to the grating that separated them from the inside. They walked back down the steps.

Shintaro's happiness was marred by one worry. Maximilian's return; the fear that she would not go on loving him living with their absent provider. The jealousy he felt at the thought of Maximilian having breakfast with her or sharing a mailbox seized him.

There was no escape. "Is it true you and Maximilian finished Harvard?" he asked.

"Yes."

"And that's where you met?"

"Yes."

He knew he shouldn't ask, but he had to know. "How?"

"On a day like today. I was afraid to go back to school that year. That made me angry at everyone. I must have come across as an incredible snob. People were nice to me, but I pretended I didn't see them."

He felt his blood rise. He unbuttoned his jacket without interrupting her. She pulled her sweater tighter around her and remembered the first time Maximilian had come up to visit her in her room at Harvard. She had tried to blow him off, but he invited himself in. "I asked him if he wanted to play a game," she told Shintaro.

"Sure," he'd said. He said he was a poker player. "I made $100,000 beating rich South Africans last year."

"You took a year off?"

"Yeah." Maximilian sat on her bed and told her about Africa.

He leaned on his elbow. She shuffled a deck of cards. "Why didn't you stay there?" she asked. "I read that the Ibo women of Nigeria considered it humiliating to be the only wife."

"Yeah."

They played poker. She won the first hand.

"Let's play again," he said.

"No," she said. "Here, let's see if you are better at chess."

"You can't just play one hand like that."

She held out her hands. He picked white. He was muscular. "Checkmate," he said.

"I have an exam tomorrow," she lied.

"Come closer," he said.

"No," she said.

"Good night."

"Good night," she said, but he didn't move. He lay back on the pillow. He pretended to have fallen asleep. Then he said, "Even next to me you're a million miles away."

"Good night," she said again.

His eyes were closed. "I'm going to my room."

Then they hadn't slept together. Shintaro took her hand. What sickness had he caught? "Ah yes," Shintaro said. They walked through the temple grounds. "Did you make a wish?" Shintaro asked, on the path again.

"No, did you?"

"You must to make a wish."

"I forgot." She smiled.

"Are you sure?"

"Maybe," she said, and quickly added, "That's a beautiful shrine. But it's very strange."

"Yes," he said. "I think so too, and I am not a *gaijin*." He couldn't keep the anger out of his voice. Had she been Maximilian's lover?

Lois turned around and looked at him.

"Foreign," he said. They walked down the gravel path. Red leaves strewn in front of them. Lois knew that to Shintaro, she would always be an outsider. There was no need to try to explain. If he got any of it, it would be from her silence.

"I thought you knew him before." The leaves were aflame when she had met Maximilian at Harvard. She'd ridden her bicycle through Cambridge the next day. The buildings had changed over the summer, and she felt like a ghost coming back to her past. It was all different. It was healthier and more elegant. Wooden and renovated. She looked around for people she knew as she walked through the square, searching, searching against all odds. She'd been homesick abroad over the summer. Now she couldn't accept that this place that was hers would have to be re-met. The names of the restaurants had changed. The streets looked fresh. Or maybe it was her tainted New York eyes taking over where Paris eyes had left off.

She met her roommate on the steps, on her way to class, as if they'd been walking around there forever. No deaths, no pregnancies, just class. Her roommate was looking fit. She hung around Harvard auditing classes, whatever she was interested in, top of the line, for free. Maybe it was fair considering how many classes she had skipped when she was enrolled. She said, "Come to my art history class," but Lois had this feeling she'd miss something if she didn't wait in the Green House Café. Lois walked along alone. Indeed, no sooner had she bought a cup of coffee than she saw Maximilian the trader. Maxi-million lived one floor down in the dorm room under hers. She lifted up her glasses.

"Hi," he said.

Her tongue was tied.

"Why do I make you nervous?" She followed his dark curls out of the café. They had walked through the yard on one of those crisscrossed paths, not knowing that they would walk all of the others together.

"Do you think Maximilian is as intelligent as you?" Shintaro asked.

"Of course not," she said.

His spirits soared.

She had tried to educate Maximilian. She would buy him books. She found an old copy of the *Harvard Advocate* and walked to the bookstore reading poems. One was about a guy being depressed with his girlfriend. He said the sky was falling with the leaves. She looked up at the red and yellow leaves as she walked across the Kirkland House courtyard, and it was true, the sky *was* falling with the leaves. The guy from the sixties poem was worried about getting caught somewhere without any cigarettes. She wondered where the sixties guy was now. She took out a cigarette and walked on until she got to the bookstore. She rolled up the magazine and stepped inside. Now she was looking for books for Maximilian. That's how she spent her free time that semester, looking for books for Maximilian. She didn't know how he was going to read all of them. Maybe she bought them because she imagined he would always live close by. They could fuse their libraries. She would get back her investment with marginal notations and astute witticisms. The main thing was, though, that she liked imagining Maximilian reading the books as she read them. So, when she went for a walk, she browsed through bookstores. It was remote communion. Each book she opened up was like an axis, a dimension. She opened them and extracted in minute appreciations, only sensing part of their purpose. There, beyond, lay Maximilian.

It only lasted a year. Where did love go? Did it just separate from his body and float back up to the sky? It was the familiarity that did them in. Nevertheless, she hung onto Maximilian and went on buying books for him. She walked slowly down the aisle, took a detour, the scenic route, turned up another aisle that would bring her finally to her goal, when . . . someone tapped her on the elbow. Or rather, brushed her lightly. She thought about not looking. It was light enough, ambiguous enough to have been accidental, ambiguous enough for her to pretend that there had been no intention behind it. And as long as she didn't say anything, she could continue browsing through the bookstore with her impenetrably silent Maximilian. But someone was always breaking the silence. She had almost walked quite out of range when she found herself standing face-to-face with her ex-lover. Maximilian smiled tentatively. He followed her to the fiction section.

"How long are you here for?" she asked. That really meant, I thought you had already left. He knew it. They had gone out for one year, and this was how it would end. "Where are you going, Mexico?" she asked, or have those plans evaporated like everything else? she didn't say.

"I'm going to New York," he said.

"Oh?"

"I've gotta pick up some warm-weather clothes."

"Good thinking. It's hot down in Mexico." She was struggling not to scold him, was still telling herself he must have known he was ruining his life running off to Mexico with its firing squads. Trying and failing to keep the sarcasm out of her voice. But how could she be expected to pass up such an opportunity to give a little push, a little steer, now that she could understand him like a piece of Swiss cheese?

He was not Maximilian. He was too real. He looked like a real puppy with its tail between its legs with that, I-knew-you-were-going-to-say-that look. "I knew you were going to say that," he said. There it was. Requited familiarity. Maybe she was too young. He crunched down the curls above his forehead and rolled his eyes as if to say, pity me, understand me, I'm soft and fuzzy. Aren't I cute?

He wasn't Maximilian. Maximilian was working to become the next thing. "I never knew anyone who was so easy on himself," she failed not to say. She couldn't stand those droopy-eyed looks now. Did she used to think he was funny? Yes, they had laughed a lot. Now they relied on their cocktail-party etiquette.

"What are you doing?" he finally said, not because he wanted to know, but because the question was already obvious and hanging in front of them, through avoidance fully expressed.

"What am I doing? Hmm." She was turning over the three answers in her head. He would know if she lied. She'd lied before. It was the only thing that worked. "Reading," she said. He helped her look for a book. He didn't know it was for Maximilian. He left for Mexico. Or maybe he was still wandering around Harvard Square. He had been good, but she bought the book for Maximilian. Maximilian would be very enthusiastic about the books. It made her happy in a general sort of way, proved for a second that it was much more than being in love with love.

There was something to be said for being a little bit uncomfortable all the time. Just enough to keep you on your toes. To keep you up to your standards, awake. The worst of all fates had to be to sleep through life. She would never cease to be amazed by Harvard. Walking home from Widener Library later that night at midnight, half the lights in all the dorms were on. Burning the midnight oil, hanging out. People were always making discoveries. She was alive.

They got back to Maximilian's apartment. Shintaro pulled her close and held her against his body reveling in her warmth, amazed that he could be driven insane by two folds of skin. Her kiss barely touched his lips. "Goodbye," she said.

Chapter 23

─────────────── ഇ൏ ───────────────

Square

A perfect job. The lobbyist wondered if *Gaijin Bank* had sunk the first billion into the fish stock. He read the newspaper for any clues to help him plan his sting, but there was nothing conclusive. He would have to call the foreigner again.

"Jack speaking."

"Jack, my friend do you remember me?"

Maximilian looked at the phone. Where did he know that voice from? "Who is this?" he said.

"Let's not play around. You have some information."

"Look buddy, I told you I'm not interested in your scam. This call is being recorded so take my advice and watch what you say."

"Who do you think listens to the recordings from *Gaijin Bank*? Meet me in the lobby."

Maximilian hung up, and pressed a button to trace the call. The tracer was blocked. He looked around. The other traders looked back at him. It would be fun leaving the New York office. Maximilian took his colleague's green coat and headed down in the elevator. "Hold my briefcase overnight," he said to the doorman on the way out. A Japanese in a gray overcoat was waiting by the phone in the lobby. Maximilian breezed by him and out into the street. "Taxi!" he called with a French accent. He got into the cab. He watched the rear window. No one was following him. The trip to the hotel was tranquil. He opened the door to his room.

A man was waiting for him inside. "Don't bother coming in," he said. Maximilian turned around to find another goon blocking his escape. "We're going for a ride," said the second Japanese man. Maximilian felt a sharp object in his back.

A black limousine pulled up to the front door of the hotel. Another henchman jumped out. Maximilian started to yell, but no one seemed to notice the struggle. He felt a pain in his back. They stuffed a handkerchief into his mouth and pushed him into the car. The door closed. "We want to talk," the driver said. "There's no need to make a disturbance."

Maximilian spit out the handkerchief. "I'm not afraid of you. I don't want your information or your propositions. We aren't going anywhere."

"We don't have time to listen," said the other man in the front seat. "We want to get one thing straight. We've been watching you. You are a good businessman. We need good businessmen, so we've decided to hire you. From now on you work for us."

"I'm not interested."

A rattling sound cut him off as the man next to him lifted a heavy chain from the floor of the car. "We can make arrangements to help your projects along. I'm sure everything can be arranged. We have eminent connections in the music industry."

"I don't need you."

"You do now. Not a word about this to anyone, or you end up at the bottom of the Hudson River, understand? The reports you've been giving to Maami will alter slightly. From now on, you are to bring *Gaijin Bank's* stock position."

"The reports?"

"Yes. They are being redirected, so to speak."

The reports? A sly smile crept across Maximillian's lips. "Is that all?" The words sounded like a piece of crystal being arranged in a glass cabinet.

"That's all."

A few people were crossing the streets of Harlem. They didn't stop to watch as the car door opened and Maximilian was thrown out onto the pavement.

The next day, the lobbyist put his suitcase into the limo. The newspaper on the plane had the story with the endangered species list and the affected companies. It's general knowledge now. Only their stock is recovering. What's a few days, anyway? Safe in the clouds of general knowledge. Poor fish, pulled from the list.

His name, dropped from the mouths of the lobbyists, would catch in the throats of rough-skinned fishermen on the seas of Japan. They would pluck the sea's fruit. She would roll under their gentle touch. She would scatter the sunlight and yield the last of a kind as it embraced a dark chamber like an arrow shot into an enemy heart.

Maximilian watched an airplane circle over the New York skyscrapers and disappear into the clouds. On the forty-second floor, Maximilian put down the phone and finished recording his trades for the day. He had been here with Arnie for two weeks now, and he was exhausted. He rested his head on the desk for a minute.

He was running. In his dream, his feet would not move at first. There was a long corridor with many doors and mirrors and lights, but it was all dark, with manholes and smoke rising up out of them. Maximilian saw himself walking, running, flying through the smoke, pausing at each door, the first of which, he knew, contained a bar. The music was very loud. People laughing. He thought of stopping in for a drink, but no, he had to find a certain door. It was urgent. There was very little time. He passed by. The next door led to a dark and terrible place where evil dark faces lurked with studded teeth, so Maximilian tiptoed up to the door, was almost past it, when it swung open.

A hand grabbed his sleeve. He shed his jacket and went on.

The next door had a '403' on it: his and Lois's apartment. The key was in the door. Maximilian watched himself reach down for the key, lock the door, and put the key into his pocket. He laughed, a soundless laugh, although he was aware that he was dreaming, and moved on to the next door: Shintaro's classroom. Shintaro was practicing for his audition;

Maximilian could hear the boy's siren voice through the door, which, he found, was locked. Maximilian heard laughter behind him. He opened his fist: the key. He turned the lock, pushed the door open.

Shintaro turned around. His eyes widened. "Come in," he said. "Shut the door."

The room was large, the ceiling so high that he might as well be outside. Then he realized he was outside on a beach. His toes sank into the white sand, were submerged in the crash of a wave. They walked toward each other on the beach. Shintaro smiled shyly, stretched out his arms. "What took you so long?" he said, a little angry.

Maximilian mimicked Lois' voice. "I was with Maximilian."

"Never mind," Shintaro said. The anger left his voice. "What a lovely dress." Shintaro pulled the white frills close and sank his face into the soft neck. He nuzzled the dark brown curls. "I love you," he said. They walked down the beach, mesmerized by the rhythm of the waves. Two masculine hands reached through the sleeves of the white dress. They pulled Shintaro's torso close. The wind picked up. The waves soaked their shoes. Shintaro threw back his head and stared into the sun for one blinding second . . .

The phone was ringing. He lifted his head off the trading desk. "Jack speaking."

"Jack, don't mention this to any of the guys on your desk."

"What now, Arnie?"

"The SEC is here. Uh, we're talking with some members of management about suspending trading on a certain seafood stock, and we'd like to have your input, if you could meet us in conference room A."

"Is this what we came here for, Arnie?" Arnie didn't answer. It was too late to unwind all the positions. The Yakuza had confiscated the stock profits in one big fire sale, and Maximilian could not un-confiscate it. "I'll be there when I finish here. Fifteen minutes." He hammered the phone down onto the desktop. If he told the SEC that a huge buy order went through just before the announcement, and another enormous sell order two days later, the Yakuza would kill him. He had the feeling he had been here before; he couldn't un-confiscate it. What was next? It was hidden in a veil of sleep. Arnie was on his own. Maximilian left the office. He left the country, this time.

Chapter 24

Plan B for Boy

Lois kept her morning ritual in Maximilian's mansion. After breakfast, she went outside to look at the sky. The sun hung low on the horizon. Another crisp autumn day was beginning. A nice day for a journey.

Alone in Maximilian's house, Lois closed the shades. Half the time she opened the shades to look out, and the other half, she drew them shut to keep people from looking in. Like a pretty girl with her glasses, she peeked through the shades, like a woman with her husband.

An earth tremor started. She ignored it and lifted the plastic off of her easel. There was her painted queen, ready for her journey to Europe. The long white dress of her abstract lady waved in the wind as she walked around the Vatican. She must have been a powerful queen, the sort to be asked by a dictator who had gathered all the men together in a line and pointed to the queen, saying, "Which one out of all shall live by your hand?"

You know which one, she said, in power, enslaved, without hesitation.

"You are beautiful," Lois said. "My painted queen, do you see me?"

She felt the Queen's presence.

How can I see you without my eyes?

They were vessels *communicants*.

The earth stopped shaking. Lois had already squeezed out the colors. She sat down and stared past the canvas. There was really only one subject. The rhythm of the brush. The story weaved itself through her hand. The story of a kingdom in a valley on a continent across the ocean. Where the ambassador said what Charles Louis Napoleon wanted to hear. The ambassador to Mexico, Napoleon's puppet. The voice told Lois to paint the valleys black. Napoleon believed the French would be welcomed by the people of Mexico. The black painted valleys were low down in the depths of everything where daylight never touched them. Napoleon agreed. Mexico would readily accept Europe's monarchial institutions. France scrutinized all the unemployed princes of Europe. Her brushstrokes grew in size and sureness and randomly touched on different areas of the canvas. It was decided at last. The Mexican crown should be bestowed upon the Archduke Maximilian of Austria.

Her strokes grew more sure. They had a rhythm of their own. The tremor ended. Yet the French troops could not easily beat Mexico back again. Bloody, the battle of Puebla. A thousand Frenchmen killed, a new national holiday for the Mexican calendar, May 5, 1862. Cool October in Austria. A delegation of exiles came to the castle of Archduke Maximilian to solicit his services as emperor of Mexico. Maximilian replied, poised on one condition. *The people of Mexico must vote for me.*

She stared at the canvas. The voice went on revealing itself. She lit a cigarette, blew a stream of smoke. It was the story of an emperor and empress in a land far, far away across the sea. The smoke hurled itself at the canvas and exploded against the surface. The smoke cleared. The colors harmonized.

And vote they would: everywhere the French army court-martialed or terrorized Liberal sympathizers and organized votes for Maximilian. Maximilian was notified that by an overwhelming majority he had been elected Emperor Maximilian of Mexico. No one but you, Maximilian, destined to atone for the sins of your sponsors, you walked into the web. You could not meet the clergy's demands to un-confiscate estates, nor Napoleon's to repay him the stolen profits from governments past. But you could die before a firing squad on the outskirts of Querétaro still eager to abolish injustice and help the oppressed. You were sublime.

There had been no tempests in your Austrian palace. And here, every little dispute, resolved in bloodshed. Your wife's skin, so white, enduring the Mexican sun. The white queen, stained though she was, loving a dead man. Tainted queen running black with bitterness; she wanted this place for you, Emperor Maximilian, by her side, nothing less.

Out of the darkness came the lady in the white dress. Not really a lady, but she was white. And there was a dark square at the queen's feet; it was the gate, and it was also a man, Maximilian, in the story at least.

And in front of the dark gate that was Maximilian was an orderly garden. It was said that on the voyage to the New World, Maximilian compiled a manual of court etiquette. Everything seemed disconnected without respect to form. The gate was supposed to lead into the garden, but it didn't come across that way; instead, the three were stacked up again like a totem, the garden on the bottom, the queen on top, and the black doorway that was Maximilian in the middle. A six-hundred-page volume on court etiquette. The most complete work written on the subject. The emperor and empress dwelt in an old Spanish castle surrounded by the cypress trees of their Aztec predecessor, Montezuma. What banquets they held the first six months. The wine bill alone! Until Napoleon tied your purse strings, Maximilian. With no money, you projected the beautification of Mexico: new highways, architecture, gifts, volumes of refined laws, codes of regulations for the navy you would one day build, the modern school systems, the abolition of servitude. You made many enemies.

From the depths, the great will climb. Great people, great deeds, the Sisyphans will stand again unstraining and free, if only briefly, on the mountaintops. He was later accused of being a hundred times more liberal than the Mexican Liberal Party he'd checked. Rome threatened to denounce him. So it was when the North Americans unexpectedly won the Civil War and wanted the French out of Mexico. Then came Bismark's Prussia, and Napoleon needed his army at home. *Draw lines from one mountain to the next and describe the map of life.* Napoleon liquidated the Mexico project. A ring of *guerrilleros* armies advanced on the capital.

Lois listened to the voice tell how she would never see Maximilian again except through veils and shadows. She watched her fingers wrapped around the brush painting the colors to the soft voice of the white queen. But to the white not queen but empress, abdication was cowardice; *she*, a vessel, would go to Paris and convince Napoleon. *My body, the queen, thins always into a dissemblance by process of elimination, chips away at the tiny shape of my magnificent fear.* As bodies do, hers cascaded piece by white porcelain piece into unrememberedness, the dark background. *How lovely your painting is.* The journey was hard. Napoleon was sick but gave her an audience thrice. Napoleon wept. They had all been duped by the promise of Mexico, that backward unsalvageable land. He would not sanction holding Mexico. She was losing her self-control. She went to beseech the Pope. The horsemen of Dürer's Apocalypse woodcuts dominated her imagination. She became obsessed with the idea that Napoleon was plotting to poison her. She was so afraid of it, she refused to leave the Pope's palace. For the first time in history a woman officially slept at the Vatican.

Lois painted a golden chalice overflowing with wine, and the queen's delicate white hand to hold it. All the next day she refused to eat or drink anything but the time she herself drew from the public fountains. The queen would sip the days as they filled her cup. The square had gotten into the chalice, and the more she tried to get it out, the larger the square grew. Though the queen had guarded it with all her might from the slayer, she could not save her golden chalice. It ran black with a bitter drink to which she soon became all too addicted, and which she could not sip slowly. It was clear to Lois, the queen was out of proportion.

As she painted, the song went on. The images were the mountains you made of the paint. The background pierced the image painted over it as if to jump into her divine eye. Napoleon urged abdication, not wanting Maximilian's death to fall on France. Maximilian hesitated in Orizaba and took up the study of botany and entomology and butterfly chasing. The French troops left; Maximilian was forced to stay. Half the kings of Europe petitioned the Mexican Liberals to release Maximilian, who meanwhile rejected all escape plans. Maximilian taught his foreign interventionist backers a lesson they would never forget. It was on the Hill of Bells that Maximilian faced the Liberal firing squad. The news of Maximilian's execution reached Paris during the Universal Exhibition.

Lois put down her brush. One side of Maximilian was still longer than the other. No matter how she worked to justify his faults, Maximilian was always getting bigger. He ate away at the canvas and poisoned the thrashing white queen.

Napoleon did not announce it until the day after the metals had been presented. From power to chaos, Napoleon, too, fell. The white queen never regained her sanity: she never stopped believing her dead husband to be the 'Sovereign of the Universe', the name of this last painting in Lois' series. The three lovers were stacked up on the totem, the garden on the bottom, the queen on top, with the black doorway that was Maximilian in the middle. The queen died, in 1927.

Maximilian had left a note on the coffee table weeks

ago. "Lois, tomorrow is garbage day if I don't come back."

And if you do come back, it's not garbage day?

Chapter 25

~~~~~~

Garbage Day

She pulled the shades again.

Shintaro came straight from work. They were going to the country. He helped her into her red wool coat, and they walked out to the train. The ride was pleasant holding hands out of the city and through the countryside. The sky lay in the watery rice fields.

In Shintaro's grandfather's house, Taro sat erect on the tatami floor. Shintaro's bronze hand placed a cup of tea on the altar for their ancestor to inhale. His life had been short. The winter solstice had marked the coming of a band of villagers to their humble *buraku* hidden between the mountains and the tall pines. The villagers had carried torches, ropes and knives, looking for the one who had kidnapped the beautiful daughter of the noble, Hojo. The men squatted down in a small circle off to one side of the hanging purple sash. The ancestors swayed on their feet, arms wrapped around their knees, and growled in low tones. They tried to avoid the eyes of their women as the nobility burned the *buraku*. Next morning, the people came out of the rubble to commiserate and gather anything resembling food. The ancestor's family was not among them.

Shintaro's grandfather, Taro, upheld the traditions and orderly conduct. He looked after the house spirit, who maintained authority. Protection from outsiders had always fallen into place naturally. The spirit exercised its power by simply not appearing, as long as everything transpired in an orderly fashion. Taro had always assured his grandson that everything transpired with unbroken normalcy. His evenness warranted that nothing should disarrange the generations. Yet their family had moved from one village to another. It was said that in this chaos a promise was broken. A random shifting of allegiances took place. It was said that the spirit had once appeared, disturbed from the family stones, and was forced to carry its tomb on its dogged back and follow the exiled family. The dead overtook the living by force of sorrow. Building a new abode, Taro's father saw the spirit come and engrave its path in stones, making old what was just new. It came to live in the beams of the new house and reminded them that there was no escape to freedom. There was no godless haven. So they upheld the traditions. Every night, Taro saw to it that his grandson washed the floor for the bath house spirit. He scrubbed until the lather mounted on the blue tile, and in the morning, came to drain the water in such a way that he would not see his own reflection.

Shintaro opened the door to the garden for Lois. Taro sat thinking in front of his bonsais dragging jewels from the sea, Shintaro said. The old man did not hear them. Lois stepped into the garden after Shintaro. The old man started and turned around. He bowed.

Lois bowed very low.

Taro bowed lower still.

Lois bowed even lower, only to be outdone by Taro. "It's okay," Shintaro said, and pulled her torso up.

Lois looked around. A strange aura of isolation pervaded the country home. They hadn't called ahead because there was no phone. Taro seemed to expect them nevertheless. This male family's ineptitude at receiving guests put her at ease. Shintaro didn't offer her food or drink, and Taro, rather than asking questions about her, or removing to some remote part of the house, followed them into a dark plant-filled parlor. This was the western-style room with sofas and coffee tables. She decided it was a comfortable house. Shintaro opened the shutters, and Lois saw that the room was full, not with plants, but with some sort of industrial sculptures which seemed like tools. "What are these things?" she asked.

"They are my grandfather's inventions."

"Really? They are beautiful. What are they?"

"Different things. I don't know all of them."

She approached a glass ball with two slots the size and shape of human hands. "What's this one?"

"That one is a . . . a—" Shintaro spoke to Taro in Japanese.

The old man laughed and bowed shyly. He said he was thankful that she was so polite.

"No, really," Lois answered, "I'm very interested to know what it is."

Taro commenced a lengthy explanation, which Shintaro reduced to three words: "a relatedness device."

"What does it do?"

"Yes, what does it do?" Shintaro consulted Taro again, and then said, "Its use is to help decide the debt to the other person. How much one must favor another."

"What is it for?"

"For gift-giving, or helping each other. It is for people who live in the big cities."

"Excuse my curiosity, but how does it do it?"

"It finds the common ancestor, and counts the generations."

Her eyes widened. "Can we try it?"

Taro was already answering her question in Japanese. Shintaro said. "It will tell us nothing because we know that Taro is my grandfather, and you and I are not related. He said maybe when you and Maximilian come here together, we can see if you have a common ancestor."

"No," she said, "never mind." She turned away from the invention.

Shintaro bowed, surprised. He lifted his head and turned to Taro, but Taro seemed to have understood. "They are related," the old man said.

"No, we're not," Lois said. "There is no blood relation."

She went back out to the garden. They followed her out. They looked at the bonsais.

"The knowledge is not so limited," Taro made Shintaro translate. "One can have many relations in many lifetimes. I am concerned with the extended family."

Lois sank onto a rock. Shintaro and Taro followed suit. She searched for a subject. "Do you find it hard to concentrate with Shintaro's practicing all the time?"

Shintaro winced.

Taro straightened up and said, "He is mostly quiet."

Shintaro added, "My grandfather worry about my singing."

"But you are such a good singer," Lois said.

Taro answered in Japanese.

"He say, It's not time for someone in our family to try to become famous," Shintaro said. "Taro thinks when we go forward, we also go backward in time."

"What do you mean?"

"He say it sounds like Maximilian has already begun moving backward. Like the water around a stone in the river. He hurries into the future with a blind eye to the past. He will be surprised when he finds himself in the past."

"And what about me?"

"It's the same thing, you and Maximilian. You must try not to be like him. You must go toward your past," Shintaro said. "I told my grandfather you met Maximilian at Harvard, but," Shintaro leaned closer to her, "he thinks you met Maximilian in Detroit." Shintaro looked at Taro. "He is old." The old man's head sank lower. "Taro say it's very interesting that you come from Detroit. He used to work for a Japanese automobile research. Your city was destroyed by the automobile."

Perhaps she would tell the story after all. "Don't let what I'm about to say go beyond this room."

"It has already gone beyond this room," Taro said in Japanese.

"He said, *We* won't tell anyone," Shintaro said.

Lois spoke slowly. What Taro didn't understand, she tried to provide in Japanese, and what she could not express, Shintaro translated. They grew very tired, but wanted to go on. "You're right, the city was falling apart. My grandfather and father also worked for the auto industry when I lived in Detroit. But my father was never good enough for the Japanese. There were many of our families broken by your technology. We took an orphan into our household. A boy. His parents had abandoned him. They said he was Italian, but I think he had some Asian blood in him. He was brooding. He was dark. He was fifteen when he came to stay with us in our house. I loved our house. It glows against the sky in my dreams. He couldn't wait to get in it and unpack his stuff. My father said he had to sleep in the attic. I showed him his room. I showed him how to get out of his bedroom window and onto the roof."

"There were many people in your house," said Taro.

"Yes. It was a big house. In the summer, we used to eat dinner in the courtyard with my uncle, my aunt, and my grandfather. One day, the maid was going in and out and pouring red wine into the grownups' glasses. I sat down first. They would enter and stand around. Maximilian ran in and sat next to me. But my father said, 'Over here, Mister,' and Maximilian had to crawl under the table to the exile seat. We never listened to the grownups.

"Then the next year, their talk became more

interesting. Maximilian and I would live in two different worlds. I was jealous."

"Why?"

"It wasn't fair. I'd always thought that things were the same for girls and boys. We don't make such big distinctions as you do in Japan, and then we are surprised that they exist anyway. There's only so much you can control, and then only so much you can pretend you control. I remember my aunt sitting down at the table talking to my uncle's friend.

"We asked to be excused. Inside was shady, like sleep. Maximilian and I sank into the solemn wood furniture. The windows were open. It was like your living room." They looked through the garden door at Taro's dark living room with its plantlike shapes.

"I can see it," said Taro. "What happened to Maximilian?"

"They sent him off. To boarding school, they said. They gave him a uniform and a suitcase. I watched him out the window as he got into the car."

"There are many differences between growing up in Japan and America," Taro said. They went in to drink tea and watch comics on TV. They ate boxed lunches. Then Shintaro went off to change into clean work clothes. He reappeared in the doorway. "It's time to go."

Taro and Lois stood up. "I wish *I* had a uniform," Lois said.

"Yes," Taro laughed, "He likes his uniform."

"I would like it, too. It would say what I was doing all the time, so I could do other things on the job."

"Shhh," Shintaro said, "Now you see where I practice singing."

Taro looked at them.

Lois bowed and said goodbye.

Taro bowed lower.

On the way back from the train station, they walked through the temple grounds once again, glad not to be alone, both so far away from home.

"Do you think your grandfather likes me?"

"He is surprised that he like you so much."

"Me, too." She watched her feet crunch the gravel on the path.

"I'm glad you have known Maximilian for a long time," Shintaro said. "You must be good friends."

"I suppose."

"What's that?"

"Like, 'I guess'."

"Does it mean he want to marry you?"

"Marry me! That's impossible."

"Why impossible?"

"Marry me for how long?"

Taro was lecturing about asexual mutants. If one appeared in a sexual species, it would double and soon, after two or three generations, the species would be all asexual. And then they would all want the same things. They had retired into their own complexities.

"He must loves you," Shintaro said.

"Love me? Do you love your arm? Once Maximilian was watching me in the mirror as I braided my hair—"

"Braided?" Shintaro asked.

"Yes like this." Lois took three strands of her hair and braided them together. "I was lingering over myself in the mirror. He was sitting on my father's bed.

'What would you do if we didn't have any mirrors?' he said."

"I don't know. Die."

"Exactly. You wish you lived in there with yourself instead of out here with me. Don't you?"

"I don't know. Sometimes," I lied.

He got off the bed and stood next to me in the mirror. He put his hand on my shoulder. "We look nice together in the mirror."

I pushed him away. He went to sit on the bed again. "That's not me in there," he said.

"You're nowhere," I said.

"I'm nowhere." He got up and walked over between me and the mirror. He leaned his back against the mirror, put out his hands, shrugged his shoulders, and said softly, "I'm nowhere." He took my hair and unbraided it. I was angry at him."

"Why can't you allow me to be who I am?" he said.

"I can. But not in relation to me."

"You cannot at all."

That was the extent of it. They sent him off, to boarding school, they said. They gave him a uniform and a suitcase. I watched him through the window as he got into the car without looking back. My father tried to pull me away from the window. You know as Aeneas left Carthage on his ship, he looked at the shore, aflame. Dido was burning on her wedding pyre.

Chapter 26

ೞ◌ಌ

Class Distinction

Nothing so stifling as an institutionalized conversation. Taken outside of the conversation class, it could potentially be an interesting question: What did you do Saturday night? As if the powers that be had a right to know. She didn't mean to pry, was just trying to stay awake. Lois had a hard time keeping a straight face with Shintaro there. "What did you do on Saturday?" she asked student after student. "I studied for my high school entrance exam," or, "I watched TV."

"Good!" she said. "How did you get so good in three weeks?"

"I check all the words, and then I do a sentence," the student said.

Lois turned to the next student, Shintaro.

He sat up in his chair, perplexed. She knew what he had done on Saturday night. His bronze body had pressed into hers as he descended on her neck. That's why she was wearing a white turtleneck today.

How serious he looked in a suit, she thought. She

tried not to imagine him telling the truth. She tried not to laugh.

Shintaro saved her. "I practiced singing, watched TV, and went to the bed."

"Went to bed," she said. "No 'the'."

Shintaro's face reddened. He enunciated, ". . . went to bed."

"Did you go to bed early?"

"Yes, I went to bed early," he said, and slouched back down in his chair, more serious than ever.

All the students looked a little scared now. Books were straightened, feet neatly crossed under desks, eyes glued to the floor. Faces blank as a snow-covered park. How to get through the next ten minutes. No one asked questions. No one talked. It had taken her weeks to get them to overlook the venerability of their teacher. She tried to say without authority, "The only way to learn English is to open your mouths and SPEAK." Now this fear of mistakes again.

They had just finished lesson seventeen. "O.K., open your books to lesson eighteen." Seven minutes to go, and they were starting a whole new lesson. Ridiculous. There was only enough time to confuse them. They weren't going to remember the first part of this lesson next week, and they couldn't go back and do it over again. That would be admitting an error. She tried not to look at their faces as they opened their books.

Then it was over. Lois punched out. Grabbed her coat. Left. She went to the coffee shop next door where she'd told Shintaro to wait. He was there at the table against the wall. "Hi," she said.

He looked up.

She sat down. "That was funny," she lied.

"It was very difficult."

"No, it was a breeze. Easy." What a shame that sarcasm didn't translate well into Japanese.

"Oh," he said.

The waiter carefully placed two bowls of coffee jelly on the table. They spooned it up. "Did you decide what song you're going to sing at the audition?"

"No," Shintaro said.

"Why don't you sing a song by the Rolling Stones?"

"The Rorring Stones?"

"Right."

Shintaro paid the waiter.

"Let's go outside," she said.

The clouds over the park were incredible, like something out of a bad painting. Lois gazed at their dark gray centers and perfect outlines. Nature seemed more beautiful mocking art and belittled her ambition. Lois did not want to let on that she was losing confidence in the value of aspiration, and held the paper steadily in front of Shintaro's face. Having given in to his teacher's persuasion, he struggled to read the words, swiftly fading in the half light. After each line, she stopped, and he repeated.

"I'm not waiting on a lady," she said.

"I'm not waiting on a lady," he said.

"I'm just waiting on a friend."

"I'm just waiting on a fliend."

"You have a beautiful voice. I know you'll make it," she said. Now it was too dark to read the print. She reached into her pocket and handed Shintaro a CD of the song. *For Shintaro,* was written on the CD.

He laughed.

Chapter 27

ഇന്റെ

The Audition

The morning of the audition, Shintaro woke up much earlier than usual and looked out the window. Taro was still meditating in the garden. Shintaro washed his face, put on his *yukata*. He seized the opportunity to have breakfast with his grandfather.

Shintaro heard Taro rolling a cigarette and stopped moving back and forth between the burner and the sink to open the wooden shutter in front of the window. The room filled with cigarette smoke. The window was too small and the house next door, too close. Shintaro had already unplugged the TV and poured himself a bowl of cornflakes. Taro scowled at the American breakfast cereal. "Good morning," Shintaro said.

"Good morning," Taro said. Shintaro handed his grandfather a bowl of rice.

Taro tried to switch on the TV. "It's broken again," he said.

"Yes," Shintaro said.

The old man grumbled and sat down. "You know it's not yet afternoon."

"Yes. I got up early to meet a friend downtown."

Shintaro refilled his cereal bowl. Taro pushed his rice bowl over to Shintaro. The old man looked up when Shintaro's hand disappeared without the bowl. A lock of hair hung down in front of Shintaro's eyes. He tucked it back into the purple sash Taro had given him lifetimes ago. The boy looked so much like his mother at that moment, Taro had to look away. Shintaro straightened the silk sash. "Do not think that those are your friends," Taro said. Shintaro choked on his cereal. Shintaro's aunt had told such stories about his grandfather.

"You be careful," Taro said.

Taro would never forgive him, Shintaro thought. Everything the old man had done to hide the family in the creases of the public eyelid. All about to be undone. Shintaro's name would go up in lights. There would be interviews. They would want to know everything. They would find him out, like they found his ancestor out. First they would discover that he'd changed his name: innocent enough, teen idols did it all the time. Then they'd find out his whole family had changed its name: strange. That they were untouchable. *Poof.*

Taro ate his breakfast. Shintaro did the same. He was not really hungry but had to try to be normal. He occasionally looked sideways at Taro to see if the old man had noticed anything out of the ordinary, but Taro seemed like Taro. He hadn't said much today. That meant he had gotten a new idea. Shintaro distinctly sensed the beginning of a new invention to outstrip the foreigners. The record company's third letter had come yesterday. They had offered twice as much as the last time. But he knew that Taro would never sell his inventions.

Breakfast was over. Shintaro washed the dishes. Taro found the TV cord and plugged it in. Shintaro looked at his watch. He turned to the station Taro liked and left the room.

Thanks to Maximilian, they were doing a big favor and letting Shintaro audition late. Into the city and down the street Shintaro went behind his escort's shoulder. Feeling as if he were wearing a brand on his untouchable, his *Burakumin*, face, Shintaro imagined all the stares were for himself, rather than for this bizarre friend of Maximilian, Masami. The many were always on the lookout for the few. The many had many ways. And the few were kept down. The lowliest of the low had forgotten what had gone wrong, and how to do things right. They just did them wrong, not out of malice. Out of ignorance. It was the duty of any upright member of society to keep the untouchables down. Taro had been beaten down too many times. His rights were wrong. Although Shintaro had never been discovered as untouchable himself, he believed Taro and lived in fear. He had never had any friends. There was no one he could trust. Had he brought a friend home from school it would not have been long before the neighborhood discovered that his family belonged in a *buraku*, before his grandfather's and his own lives were ruined as they had been for generations past. He had not had a friend, until he met the two Americans a year ago. Shintaro was shaking.

In the audition hall Masami carefully explained the situation to Shintaro. Maximilian had arranged it all. They just had to do what Maximilian had told them to do. "Sing the song." Masami handed Shintaro the song sheet.

"I don't like this song," Shintaro said. "It won't be good."

"Maximilian said this was an appropriate song to sing for the audition."

"It isn't for me," Shintaro said in as flat a tone as he could manage.

Masami snatched the song sheet out of Shintaro's hands, walked over to Katosan. They argued for a second. Masami returned with a new sheet, said, "O.K., can you sing any of these?"

"This one is OK," Shintaro said.

They called his name. Chills ran down his spine. He stepped onto the stage, spoke to the conductor, handed him the song sheet, turned on the microphone, trying to control the shaking.

Masami sat up in his seat. He would swallow his pride and help the boy make it, as Maximilian had asked. They had an open relationship. It was Masami who had first insisted on that, and Maximilian had already paid him back helping separate the Yamaken-gumi Yakuza gang from *Gaijin Bank*, and he would pay again when Masami's new *Namazu* Yakuza gang took profit on its boatload of fish stock. The music started. Good thing Maximilian couldn't be here: the boy looked nice in a black suit . . . but, he had to relax.

Shintaro missed his cue. The song stopped, started over again. Someone yelled something. Shintaro bent into the microphone. "Strangers in the night . . ." he sang. And sang. And thought, how easy, as the words floated from his mouth. He felt the audience's contentment. Now it was he who held sway over all. Nice! The judges had stopped taking notes, were looking up to see who was generating the sound. How easy, he was thinking as his eyes drifted out to the audience and up the aisle to the last row of seats where Taro sat frozen in the last row. He knew! Shintaro's throat contracted.

"What's wrong now?" Masami mumbled. Shintaro's eyes had lost their focus. Masami slouched down. The boy had gotten off to a good start, a really good start, but now he was losing it. Masami dropped his head into his hands. Shintaro missed another cue, laughed nervously, said, "I'm sorry."

"No," Masami yelled, "Don't stop, don't stop!" He had moved to the aisle in front of the stage, was waving his hands furiously, was shouting, "KEEP GOING!"

Shintaro sang the parts he had already sung until the music ended. His face went from red to white. He'd blown it. His muscles relaxed. Relief. He looked at the back row. Taro was gone. Shintaro walked toward Masami and Kato. "That was great!" Masami shouted theatrically. Shintaro made his way up the steps. "Wasn't he great?" Masiami said to Kato.

"Yes . . . he have a nice voice, but . . . his stage presence is not so good. And his memory of the song: bad."

"Bad," Shintaro said, approaching the two.

"Yes," said Kato.

Masami locked eyes with Kato. Masami's tattooed

hand reached into his inside pocket and pulled an envelope out. He fanned his face with it and smiled into Kato's widening eyes.

You? Kato's eyes said, recognizing the envelope, afraid of its despicable contents. Kato ran his fingers through his hair. "Stage presence," he said, "can be taught."

Masami put the envelope back into his jacket. "Shintaro is a good student," He said.

"Does Maximilian know about this?" Kato demanded.

Masami pretended not to hear. "Don't be so worried. There is no need to show them to your wife or your mistress, is there?" Masami said.

Kato bowed and left the theater.

"You're in," Masami said as they climbed the auditorium steps. "Let's celebrate. Do you want to come to my apartment for a drink?" He put his arms around Shintaro's shoulders, but Shintaro slipped out of Masami's grasp. Masami's effeminate face hardened. "We know who you are, Shintaro. We know your grandfather, and his father, too. *Burakumin* make up sixty percent of the Yakuza. You are one of us." Masami's shirt sleeve inched up to reveal the horrible sign of the new Yakuza clan.

Shintaro saw the tattoo and caught his breath.

Masami hissed. "Yes, I am *Baka*."

Shintaro stepped backward up an auditorium step, aware that Masami had sunken to the lowest level. *Baka* assassins were misfits and delinquents. Shintaro looked at the edges of the tattoo that marked these people trained from childhood by the Yakuza to silence anyone opposed the cruel dictates of gang politics. Masami was the kind of person Shintaro's family had tried hard to avoid. Shintaro sat down in the back row of the audition hall where Taro had been. "What was in that envelope?" he said.

Masami laughed, sat down next to Shintaro. "Just a little persuasion," he said.

"What persuasion?" the boy asked.

"It's nothing but a prank." Masami opened the envelope and showed the pictures of himself, Kato, a couple of other business men, and two women in a hot tub. All the faces were red with alcohol, except for Masami's. "Here, look at this one!"

Shintaro turned away in disgust. "Where did you get those?" Shintaro asked without looking at the picture Masami was jabbing into his side.

"Compliments of a mutual friend."

"That's terrible," Shintaro said. He got up.

Masami grabbed the boy's wrist. "Listen," Masami said, "Maximilian would be very disappointed if you didn't make it. I know this business stinks, but you've got real talent. None of the other singers have it. The guys who run this whole thing know nothing about music. They know marketing, brainwashing, and money. That's it. They keep everybody dumb. Everybody spends on dumb music and paraphernalia. Posters, baseball cards. Now it's your moral obligation to break into this racket . . . you see?"

"All too clear." A useful phrase Lois had taught them.

". . . to break into it, and turn it around. Make it better. The man who does it the first time sets a precedent. To do that, first you have to come down to their level, sing their stupid songs, just for a while. This is your chance. You have to take it. You have to, you owe everyone, you owe me."

"Goodbye."

Masami pushed Shintaro back into his seat. "Listen," Masami whispered loudly. "Listen, here's the next singer. Do you hear that? That is garbage! Is that not garbage?"

Shintaro's head hung over his lap. He tried not to listen, but the music was too loud, and Masami's grip surprisingly tight.

"I repeat. Is that not garbage?"

"Yes."

"Aren't you embarrassed that this is the only music coming out of your country?" Masami's eyes locked onto Shintaro's.

"No," Shintaro said. "I am embarrassed to be here with you."

Masami let the boy go. The footsteps grew fainter behind Masami. The door slammed shut. Masami's eyes slammed shut. He inhaled, exhaled, sank into his seat. His jacket hiked up around his neck. His arms hung limply at his sides. Something had gone wrong. Here he was caught in the middle again. Even Maximilian would be displeased. It wasn't supposed to happen this way. Everybody was supposed to benefit this time.

The audition was almost over. Masami found Kato and handed him the envelope full of photos. Never mind," he said, "I'm sorry."

Kato snatched the photos, said some harsh words in Japanese, breathed deeply, then added, "The other board member like the boy singing. But let me tell him; you get out of my business."

Masami bowed and left the auditorium. His stomach felt hollow. He remembered in detail the last time he'd eaten, a habit he'd picked up the year he was abandoned by his family. Now the gang was making so much money, and he had no time to buy a bowl of noodles. But the telephone had a soba restaurant next to it. He had to check on Maximilian's bank friends. Masami's stomach growled. He slid the coin into the slot.

Chapter 28

ℬℭ

Secret

His bronze fist rose to the large metal 403. His fingers opened slowly, touched the numbers. Cold. He knocked.

"Just a minute," came the voice from inside.

Shintaro straightened his jacket, realized he was smoking, put out the cigarette on the bottom of his shoe, and stuffed the butt into his pocket. The door opened.

"Hi," Lois said. "What a surprise."

Shintaro looked at his shoes.

"Um, how was the audition?" she quickly asked.

"The audition? Yes. I . . . blew it."

"Oh. I'm sorry. Are you sure?"

"Yes. I forgot the song."

"Damn. You probably didn't have time to learn it."

"No. I didn't sing that song. I sang 'Strangers in the Night'."

"You did?"

"Yes."

"Oh. Well. Come in." She smiled and opened the door.

He followed her, not knowing what else to do. She looked especially nice today. He liked her best in her work clothes. She said she never wore skirts unless she had to. He wanted to say something about how pretty her sweater was or how nice she looked in a skirt, but all he could manage was, "Oh, you got a run."

"Yeah, those subways. You know, so many people stepped on my feet. I think today is the record. I had to change stockings three times, and I was fifteen minutes late for work . . . ." The run started under her shoe and ended somewhere above her hemline.

Shintaro began untying his shoes.

"No, no, keep your shoes on. I've decided this is an American apartment. The floor's dirty. Never mind. Come on."

"Are you sure?"

"Yes, it's O.K. The floor is very dirty."

"Oh."

"It's tea time. I'll make some tea."

"Thank you."

Lois went off to the kitchen. Shintaro walked around the apartment in his shoes. There was really nothing to it. Large space, large windows, nothing on the walls except a black painting with Lois's name on the bottom. He stared at this.

Lois returned with two cups and a pot of tea. "Oh. Don't look at that."

"Sorry I wasn't . . . . Why?"

"It's no good."

"Is it yours? I mean, did you?"

"Yes, I painted it."

"It's . . . what is it?"

"Some people who . . . have a lot of trouble keeping their feet on the ground."

"They lives in the Floating World."

"They live."

"They live."

"Yes," she said. She sat on the couch and poured the tea. "I thought your generation didn't know about that stuff."

"Yes. But my grandfather love that stuff."

"Yeah? What else?"

"I don't remember, just you can leave the Floating world by . . . medi —"

"Meditation."

"Yes. Meditation."

"Or death?"

"Yes. But that's not . . ."

"Practical."

"Plactical?"

"What else does he say?"

"He think Japan is under the 'Curse of the Green Snake.' It's Mishima. My grandfather likes the military."

"And what is the 'Curse of the Green Snake'?"

"I don't know that word in English."

She handed him the dictionary. Shintaro sat down, took a sip of tea, and flipped through the pages. "The theory or doctrine that 'p' 'h' 'y' 's' 'i' 'c' 'a' 'l'. What's that?"

"Physical." She tried to touch his chest, but he turned away.

"Physical well-being and worldly possessions con . . . constitute the greatest good and highest value in life. That's 'materialism'."

"Hm. Maybe it's a good thing that you're not going to become a teen idol."

"Yes, my grandfather must think so."

"Does he know?"

"Yes, he discovered it today. But he doesn't know I failed at the audition."

"You didn't tell him until today?"

"A kind of."

"Why not? I mean, I don't really think he'd be that angry considering that it's the only way to become a singer in Japan."

Shintaro took a sip of tea. He was blushing. "Yes," he said, and said no more.

Lois leaned forward over the table. "Well why then?"

"It's very difficult," Shintaro said.

"Fine. I like difficult things."

"You can't understand it."

"Come on, that's not fair; you're not trying." She set her cup loudly down on the table.

Now Shintaro almost wished he hadn't come, was about to make an excuse to leave. His hand reached for the dictionary instead. After looking up a couple of words, he closed the dictionary, put it down on the table, and repeated something a few times under his breath.

"What?" Lois said.

"American people are free to invent his own past."

Lois thought about that for a minute. "So?"

179

"So, Japanese are not."

"I don't get it."

"Told you," he said.

There were certain things she wished she'd never taught him. "Come on." She sighed, drew back her hair and tried again. "That's too vague. You have to apply it."

Shintaro picked up the dictionary. He looked up 'vague,' and 'apply.' "'Apply' is like 'plactical'?"

"Yes."

"I see." His eyes drifted from the page to his fingertips, and followed the bones of his fingers up to his wrist. Three o'clock, his watch read. He lifted it to his face. "It's late. I better go." Shintaro stood up.

"Wait a minute," Lois said.

Her eyes were big and deep.

"How are we supposed to be friends if you don't trust me?" she asked. "Friends trust each other."

Shintaro opened the dictionary again. *Trust: firm reliance on the integrity, ability, or character of a person or thing; confident belief; faith. Reliance on something in the future; hope. To have confidence in. To believe . . . .* He closed the dictionary, was silent for a long time.

The telephone rang, one, two, three . . . eleven times. Shintaro looked up at Lois to see if she was going to answer it, but she just stared at Shintaro.

"O.K., I trust you don't tell ANYONE. Even Maximilian." Shintaro's breathing was hard.

"I promise," she said.

"Because I never told anyone. Not even Japanese, or Maximilian. You promise?"

"I said I promised. Don't you believe me?"

"But this is real. No jokes."

"I'm not joking."

"O.K., well . . . ." He drained his cup. "Can I have some more tea please?"

She poured him another cup.

"A long time ago, before the Tokugawa Emperors of Japan — do you know about them?"

"Yeah, sort of."

"Those were the emperor who kept the peace for hundreds of years. But before them even was a —" He looked up a few words in the dictionary, "a class of people called . . . *burakumin*." Shintaro took a deep breath. He was surprised at himself for saying that word. "Do you know what that mean?"

"No."

"Oh." Relief. He could still leave and be safe. The words forced their way to the surface: "That mean . . ." He looked into the dictionary. ". . . that mean 'untouchable'." He fell silent. His hands were shaking.

"I don't see what that has to do with anything."

"Don't you see? 'Untouchable' is the worst thing in the world. No one can discover that."

"You mean your family was untouchable?"

"I mean 'was' and 'is', are the same in Japan. 'Untouchable' is dirty, not clean, like animals, people thinks." Now he was shaking uncontrollably all over. "I am untouchable. That's what I mean. I AM UNTOUCHABLE." He turned his back to her.

Lois set down her tea cup, walked over to him. "Come on, that must have been so long ago. You are beautiful. Those silly superstitions don't apply to you." She put her arms around his shoulders.

He started, pushed her away. "Don't touch!" he said.

"Look, I don't believe those things. They're not true."

"No, you will be dirty."

"I'm already dirty," she said, stepping in front of him.

"This is not a joke." He turned away again.

Her voice was small. She said, "Let me hug you."

Shintaro stared at his feet. She pulled him close, wrapped her arms around his neck and squeezed him hard.

He stood frozen. The thin white arms finally around him. And she might as well be getting her feet stepped on in the subway as he lay in his futon. Might as well be teaching his English class. Or flirting with Maximilian. "You don't understand," he whispered. She might as well be in America.

"No, you don't," she said, and laughed, still holding him tight against her breast.

He did not cry.

The phone rang again. "Answer it," he said.

Lois answered it. "Hi Maximilian . . . . Yeah, I heard it didn't go so well . . . . Really? That's great! . . . . No, no, he's here. Yeah. I'll let you talk to him. Just a minute." She set down the receiver. "Shintaro, Maximilian is on the phone."

"I . . . don't want to talk." He turned his face to the window.

"Just for a second? He has some news."

"No."

"Please?" She handed him the receiver.

"Hello what."

182

"Sorry," Maximilian said.

Shintaro held his breath.

"SORRY!" Maximilian said. "I didn't know about the photos. It was Masami's little prank. I guess he took it too far."

Shintaro listened.

"I don't want to argue with you. There'd be no one on my side. Look, Masami gave those photos back to Kato. He'll tell you. Kato said he wants you anyway. Are you listening?"

"Yes."

"You're supposed to go to his office on Tuesday. I gave Lois the address. Got it?"

"I understand what you said."

"Well are you going?"

"I don't know."

"I know how you feel. I really am sorry. I don't know what Masami could have been thinking. O.K.?"

Shintaro exhaled.

"Well, put Lois on."

Shintaro watched Lois take the phone, heard Maximilian's voice, "Is he going to do it?"

"What?" Lois asked.

"Be a teen idol."

"How should I know? They have to offer it to him first."

"They will. I'm gonna give them a great stock tip. What they're going to make on fish stock will cover the cost of promoting 'Tomorrow'." Although Maximilian didn't like giving away his best stock tip, the idea of Shintaro failing the audition was unacceptable. He deserved to succeed, and Maximilian had to make sure it happened. Once the boy had the deal under his belt and had built up a little self-confidence, things would be different. They would both be comfortable, and then they'd see how they felt. "Come on. I know he talks to you. Is he going to accept? What's going on with him? Tell me the truth."

Shintaro slipped through the apartment door. He walked down the street humming the hunt song quietly to himself.

Shintaro sang, and lo! the falcon, as it burrowed into the snow. They sang the falcon hunt song as they marched back down the trail to their village. The untouchables. They hung the game on the pole at the center of the houses. The ancestor warmed himself by the fire pit. They told stories. It seemed a young girl had saved the life of a samurai with a blade of grass. When it was the ancestor's turn, he simply unfolded his wonderful sash. The hunters stared. He hung it on the pole with the shiny falcons. What luck. They sang. As if it were alive, the purple sash flew with the singsong on the wind. Its silken skin captured the red and orange fire in its coolness, like the hottest of flames, like a tongue, like a flag hailing the great cause of the world. Indeed, there were many spirits hovering beyond the halo of fire, and as their number increased, the youths felt their boundlessness. It was the day of remembering dead souls. The sash fluttered triumphantly as if heralding a long-forgotten spirit. The men fell silent. Such a sash could only belong to royalty, and was not for them. Each knew the others' fear. They could answer only with their own, and disbursed. Shintaro sang in a low voice as he walked along.

Autumn was something Shintaro knew, with its golden leaves. Autumn made Shintaro feel he should be back at school. He was wearing his burgundy sweater. He had told her. He got out of the station and rode his moped along the country road under a tunnel of trees with a feeling of enormous well-being. He felt for the first time that no matter what happened, he would be all right. His bike dipped into a puddle. He splashed the leaves on the roadside. He rode on into the sunshine past a field. He felt extraordinarily safe, with such a high level of *ki,* that he wondered if the energy had gathered around him because of some impending danger. But why shouldn't he be all right? He knew he was not alone. He felt a presence, and expected to see his ancestor when he looked into the mirror on his handlebars. No one, of course. He vaguely wondered what was going to happen next, but he felt so reassured by the presence that he didn't question it. He was already on the road. The trip would be long. He came to the end of the woods, and turned off the dirt road and onto a main road. When he arrived at the house, the angel had gone.

Chapter 29

———————————————ৡৎ———————————————

Tomorrow

Winter fell. Rumor swept through the city, tearing down slogans, changing the popular colors from pink and Day-Glo green to black and indigo blue, scratching yesterday's starlets off bedroom ceilings. Shintaro received the letter from the record company. They agreed to sign him on. All he had to do was stamp his *hanko* on the form and he could make a CD with them.

He hid the letter under his dresser, dimmed the lights, and stood in front of the mirror. He *was* good-looking. He knew that he could do it.

But if he signed on, someday they would find out that he was untouchable. He couldn't help being angry at Maximilian, trying to expose their family. Shintaro took the letter back out. He found his name seal in his top drawer: Tomorrow had arrived.

"Tomorrow!" His name swept through the city, as the baseball cards, T-shirts, and buttons fell from Rumor's talons.

Shintaro learned many things. He could play air

guitar while he sang. He completed his how-to-be-a-teen-idol crash course. He made his first CD. All the songs were composed by salarymen. He had agreed to sing their songs on his first CD under the condition that they let him write half of them on the next one. He was sure they would refuse, and he would be free. They had not refused. Now, his first CD was selling more than expected. "I have songs to write in English," Shintaro told Lois as they slowly walked to her language school.

The boss paced the corridor frantically. This was the last time. He was not going to teach her class this time. The students needed to understand why he was letting her go. Through the classroom window, he watched them sitting patiently in a circle. He made a show of looking at his watch and pacing up and down.

Lois arrived twenty minutes late with Tomorrow. Her boss snarled in her ear, "I want to see you after class." He ushered them into the classroom. As soon as the girls recognized their classmate as the famous teen idol Tomorrow, they started screaming with their fists in front of their mouths. The boss looked around to see who was to blame. Lois held onto Tomorrow's arm to keep him from passing out. Only when three boys rushed up to Tomorrow with papers and pens for his autograph did the boss begin to understand. With acrobatic celerity he played off Tomorrow's condescension in their classroom as his own idea. He shook both Lois' and Tomorrow's hands three times.

A music video was ready and waiting for Tomorrow to step into the central role, and was recorded in a few days. Shintaro missed it on TV, but when he walked into a bar near the studio, everyone yelled, "It's Tomorrow!"

The result of Shintaro's success was an immediate lack of privacy which extended to everyone he knew. They gave up on disguising themselves to go out. Maximilian had plenty of money to spend, but he and Lois stayed at home. He did the shopping and she did the cooking.

Maximilian was surprised at the sudden rush at their local supermarket. There was a crowd around one of the refrigerators. People were bantering in Japanese at the back of the line holding up packages of frozen fish. There was the familiar character for Tiki. Maximilian could make out the word 'Tiki' in peoples' banter in the frozen food section.

Maximilian put the frozen fish down on the counter and announced, "I'm going to travel around for a while."

"And leave us here alone?"

"Things are getting sticky at the office. Not everything that goes on there is above board."

"Don't be a catastrophist. You're not involved in that, are you?"

"Involved or not, they're always looking for a scapegoat. I'm low enough down on the food chain to be expendable but high enough to know what's going on." He left her a wad of bills in the hall drawer, "just in case," and asked, "Will you miss me when I'm gone?"

"Not as much as I miss you when you're here," she

said. Then she looked at him seriously in the eyes. "Tell me again. This secret new branch of the Yakuza, the Namazu, is struggling for power with the Yamaguchi-gumi. And they're the largest and wealthiest Yakuza gang?"

"Yeah, but it's more than a struggle. It's an all-out war. They're competing for billions of dollars a year from extortion, gambling, the sex industry, guns, drugs, Internet pornography, real estate and construction kickback schemes, and yes, stock market manipulation. The only explanation I can think of is that our bank has been paying homage to Yamaguchi-gumi for a long time, and now the rival clan wants in. Look, I've got to get out of here. Don't worry. You'll be safe, as soon as I'm gone."

Maximilian sent a postcard from Saudi Arabia. Lois kept the shades closed all the time now when she was home alone. She woke up late. It was cloudy and rainy outside. The night before, she'd felt she was making no progress. Everything looked ordinary. She went to the study and looked in the mirror: she looked great. Her face was smooth, her figure perfectly curved. She would take her cues from the physical. She went into the kitchen and opened the window.

Maximilian was back from his travels. "He's my Maximilian," Lois said.

"No, he's my Maximilian," Shintaro said. He picked up Maximilian's suitcase and carried it out of the station.

"What's for dinner?"

"I'm thawing out those Tiki fish," Lois said.

"You will be amazed at his progress," Lois said the next day. They were on their way to meet Shintaro at his studio. They knocked on the star's door. "Come in." Tomorrow was dressed in red, black and yellow satin and bore a striking resemblance to Elvis. They went into a dimly lit lounge area. Tomorrow's manager was there, yelling at a roadie, "What are you doing?"

"This is the best way to mike up a kick drum."

"Drop that and go get us some sushi."

The shiny figure stood against the window looking out; Shintaro turned around. "Hey!" Maximilian said. "Check out those threads."

Shintaro said he was getting ready for an interview. "Interviews are easy," Maximilian said. "The first thing you do when you walk into the room is decide which people are the sacrifices and which are the audience, and act accordingly."

"Right," Shintaro said. "'Accordingly?'"

Maximilian mimed an accordion player.

"Oh, I see," Shintaro said.

"You do not," Lois said. "Where's your dictionary?"

"At home."

Someone came in to announce that it was time for the interview. Shintaro excused himself. "Where will you be?"

"I'm taking Lois shopping for a white dress," Maximilian said. Then we'll go back to the house. Why don't we meet for dinner?"

"I'll try," Shintaro said. He didn't look at Lois.

Outside, Lois took Maximilian's arm. "Saudi Arabia, huh?"

"Yeah. It was exactly the same as last time."

"You aren't, though. Why did you buy that jacket?"

"It loved me, and I felt sorry for it," Maximilian said in his full-length leather jacket. "Lois, my dear, even you can't make me sad today. You are wondrous. An angel disguised as a woman. I'd never have believed it if I hadn't seen it with my own eyes."

"What do you want, Maximilian?"

"I was just getting to that. I want to take you shopping. I know you've been coveting it for a long time, and honey, you deserve that white dress."

"I can be bought and sold, but I will always steal myself away, you criminal," she said.

"This is legal. Here's the plastic. All we have to do is ascend into the department store."

They escalated from the train station to "My King." Up, up, up into that Eden of new-smelling fashions waiting to be plucked. The theme for the day was white. Accessories first, since they had a better chance of fitting. White hats and gloves. White scarves and muffs. "The muff is key," Lois said. Then on to the dresses. After several trials and errors, the fact was plain. None of the dresses fit her lengthy body. "I know I'll fit into this white fox fur coat."

"That wasn't in the deal," Maximilian said.

"I'm beginning to think that dress doesn't exist. Let's go home. I didn't want it anyway. I wouldn't be myself in it. The muff's nice. Thanks a lot, Maximilian."

"Thank you for taking care of my apartment. Sorry we couldn't find the dress."

"No problem, partner."

"Partner?" he said.

"Yeah."

On the way back to the *mansion*, Maximilian pumped her for information on Shintaro. Lois said she had seen very little of Shintaro recently. He had cancelled his English classes. No more going to department store photo exhibits, coffee shops or record libraries. They never got to see half of the movies they'd rented. They didn't get to Akihabara. Shintaro ended up buying a new stereo at a more expensive store near Aoyama. Maximilian looked dejected. "He wants to move into your place, too," Lois said. "He needs a place near here, not far from the shrine." She didn't mention that she and Shintaro had kept up their walks near Harajuku. Shintaro wore a hat and sunglasses. "He likes the view of Tokyo from your apartment. I don't know if he likes the way it's decorated, though."

"Change it," Maximilian said.

The apartment would have character furnished with Taro's gadgets. Taro's goodbye presents to Shintaro. Talismans. A self-gardening and temperature control unit, mirrors that changed color. It would be a self-sustaining *mansion*.

Shintaro didn't make it to dinner that night. He finished late and went back to the country to rest. Shintaro knew that his grandfather was all but disowning him. He stayed in the country as long as he could, and then prepared for the move to Tokyo. On his last day in the country, they played *Go* in the living room of Taro's house. The moving truck would be there soon.

"Remember your ancestor," Taro said. It was the day of remembering of dead souls. Shintaro looked out at the statues in the rock garden.

Shintaro won at *Go*. The old man scooped up the pieces, and put the game in one of his grandson's boxes. Shintaro went out to the garden. He sang his new hit single, changing a few notes and slowing the pace to add a new dissonance and irregularity. He sang as if out of nowhere, like the sash from the sky, here at home for the last time. He sat alone in the garden. His ancestor had been staring at the purple mountains behind his garden, sipping the same five o'clock pitcher of sake he had been sipping for the past fifty-one years when the Americans came to his hometown in Chiba and changed life as it had been known to his family for the past hundred years.

The ancestor went on sipping his sake, that day and the next, though now sometimes accompanied by one of the more intelligent soldiers, John Mackinney, who had picked up a bit of Japanese since he had first set foot on Japanese soil a year earlier. The ancestor was eager to learn the American's ideas about living because Americans didn't require that the *burakumin* kneel down in the street as they passed. They didn't mind touching *burakumin's* hands when receiving change or saying hello. And Americans had such powerful magic. The ancestor's wife managed to look the other way. Each time she brought another pitcher of sake to the two at the table in the garden, she kept her eyes on the ground. The ancestor was enraptured by Mackinney's stories and demonstrations of American gadgets and weapons. They exchanged many presents. Much to the disgust of the female members of the family, the ancestor managed to pass his fascination with Western magic on to his son, Taro, grandfather of Shin — 'new' — Taro.

And now the new American came with the truck. Maximilian descended from the driver's seat and stood facing Taro. They bowed. Taro packed the gadgets in boxes and put them in the moving truck himself.

In a press conference, Tomorrow enchanted the public with his scientific origins and his soft-spoken strength, demonstrating some of his grandfather's magical gadgets.

Chapter 30

───────────── ℘℧ ─────────────

The Shadow

The boss clenched his tattooed fists and snarled at Masami. "We urged you to have your own legitimate business. We allowed you to have your own subsidiary family. Now you have been elected as underboss. It's time to take a leadership role. Make a stand in the war on the Yamaken-gumi." He nodded at the dark shadows in the back of the room. Two men stepped forward and seized Masami's arms.

"You have chosen wisely, teacher. There is no need for persuasion. I have already extracted the information from the American. Rest assured that Yamaken-gumi's foreign bank front is saturated in Tiki fish stock, Zamzen, PetroAmic, and all the others. They have over a billion in targeted shares. It's time."

The boss threw back his head and laughed. The bodyguards slipped back into the shadows.

Lois walked out of her painting and into the grounds of Meji Jingu Shrine followed by Shintaro, who tilted his head back. "I have felt very sad," he said.

She looked at him. He did look upset.

"This is for you. It's a present from Taro." He handed her a cloth-wrapped package. They sat on a bench. She opened it and took out a white silk kimono. "Oh my." *The white queen.* "How did he know I was looking for a white dress?"

"He know everything."

"Thank you. Thank Taro for me." She hugged him. He drew back. She laughed and put the kimono in her giant shopping bag. "I will paint it."

"Paint it! What color?"

"White, of course. I'll need someone to model it, though. Do you think you could wear it? Just for an hour?"

Shintaro looked at her childlike face pleading with him. He could not say no. He took her hand.

"Life has changed a lot for you," she said at length.

"Yes. How do you feel?" he asked her.

"I don't know." Her voice trembled. "Alone. Weak. There are some ideas that are so beautiful that I keep trying to believe in them no matter how many times life proves them unsustainable. Like with Maximilian. I do the same thing again and again expecting a different result."

"What do you mean by Maximilian?"

"Maximilian is hopeless because he is younger than me by one year."

"So am I. Does age matter?"

"Youth always seems to have the upper hand in a

relationship. The youthful always get the best. A woman who marries a younger man is made to give everything and then buried in a full house. Whereas marrying an older man is like finding a patron of the arts and an empty house."

He looked at her doubtfully.

"I don't know," she said. "The only thing left to do is not eat."

"American girls always diet. You come from a good family. You don't need a patron."

"But what do you inherit coming from a 'good family'? There are many things to learn. That which does not come about by choice does not come about, and then there is no avoiding death."

Shintaro thought about this. "We must assume existence, even as heirs."

"I think that someone who changed to virtue is more good and more wise than someone who knew the laws naturally," she said.

"That is a sacrifice."

"And the alternative?"

"Love," he said.

"A few years after being consumed there is nothing left to love. There is necessity. Fear of loneliness. There are memories. One song said I'd rather have a memory than a dream. But I don't know. At least a dream can still happen."

They walked on. "I don't know how I can face this mediocrity."

"What's 'mediocrity'?"

"Not good, not bad."

Above them, a V of geese flew across the sky. "I

see." He saw the sky, bigger than the hole in his heart.

"I don't think Maximilian is coming back this time," she said. "Have you ever felt a dread of a danger coming, hanging over you, that you can't pinpoint? Have you ever felt your thoughts darken like a sunny day that has gone black ahead of a storm? You turn your family and friends over in our mind asking, Where? Who? And it won't be long before you know the answer."

"He always come back." Shintaro looked sadder than ever.

"What's wrong with you?" Lois said.

"I don't know. I feel like a different person when I speak English."

"More free?"

"Maybe. You know the 'shin' in Japanese means 'new'," he said.

"Yes, New Taro," she said. "When I speak Japanese, I feel like this incredibly polite person. I always define myself in terms of certain levels within society. I'm always conscious of my position."

They walked through the gate of the shrine, and up the temple steps. Shintaro reached into his pocket and pulled out two ten yen pieces. He handed one to Lois. "My grandfather has died," he said.

"No!" Her hand tightened into a fist around the coin.

Shintaro threw the coin through the grating. He clapped his hands together and made a wish.

"I'm sorry." She saw he could not cry.

He bowed his head.

She held the white kimono. Graceful transpiration, white dress.

They walked back out of the garden into the Floating World. "I feel my grandfather's *ki*."

"What's *ki*?"

"His energy. Life source, strength. I think he is here."

"Do you think so? It must be hard to let go."

"Trying to convince people to think like you drains their courage to think for themselves. We must not take peoples' *ki*."

"That sounds like your grandfather."

The sky had turned gray. The streets of Aoyama boiled with rain. They ran under a tree.

"When did you see him last?" Lois asked.

"I see him every day. He lives in our house among our family's house spirits. He protects the house and the family."

"The world has imposed itself enough on you. Men. Maximilian, too. All these roles to fulfill. The only consolation is that you have a part. And woman's only consolation is that we are free."

"The funeral was yesterday. I watched the dust rise from the earth. It was my last chance to pay him back. I betrayed him. I was not supposed to become famous. I was not able to save him, only hurt him. Then the funeral procession went out of the cemetery. I escaped. I left for a new identity. I escaped my identity and my punishment. Our family should have waited for more generations to come out. Now Taro is dead, and there is no punishment great enough for Tomorrow."

Chapter 31

————————————&)Q————————————

Labyrinth

The newscaster's falsetto rose above the hundreds of protesters in back of him on TV. "The ruling to take the Tiki manta ray off of the endangered species list has been overturned following an investigation into stock manipulation by the known Yakuza gang, Yamaken-gumi."

Arnie doubled over.

"Get that garbage can!" Joe yelled.

There went his yacht in the Mediterranean, his house in Cambodia, his mistress.

Several of the boys slumped into their chairs. Maximilian watched his profits melt to nothing and below. The phones were ringing. The line crackled. "We have to help you out of this position. Your P&L is negative five million." He had hit the pavement. The other stocks in the portfolio began to cascade as the Namazu took their money off the table. The next two days marked a long, torturous slide. Ambitions crashed. There would be a heavy adjustment of expectations on the trading floor.

Maximilian stayed home and tried to forget. Through an arrangement of paper doors, the three friends managed to separate their apartments. Lois had taken the eastern room, Maximilian, the western, and Shintaro, the southern. It was like living at school. She set her easel up on the terrace in the morning. Taro's gadgets populated half of the living room. Maximilian, their fighter, a pillar of strength in their community, came and went. Lois lived in the community she depicted. She struggled with its disjointed fabric trying to link its elements. She prevailed upon Shintaro to wear her pink lipstick and captured his soul in paint swirling in the white kimono.

The news spread by word of mouth. Now there was a crowd of people hoping to be comped in the street outside of Sazzae. The bouncer spotted Lois and Maximilian near the back and pointed at them. The waters parted, and the two skirted into the club. Familiar faces asked about Tomorrow. "He's at the studio, where else?" It was too crowded, and Masami was too busy helping the bartender make money behind the bar to lavish his free drinks on them.

Lois went back home with Maximilian's two-dimensional self. He posed. He was her subject. They were perfect. Perfect strangers. Around two a.m., he would roll into her internal dialogue. "What are you doing on my side of the apartment?" she would say.

"How's it going, cupcake?" he asked.

She was fast-forwarding through an art film.

His dress shirt was unbuttoned and hanging loose over faded jeans. She marveled at the hair on his chest as he picked up a magazine and read.

"That won't work on me," she said.

The next night he was turning the pages of the magazine. "One look from you is all I expect out of a day," he said.

"I don't know how long I'm going to last here," she said.

"Vas y, à Paris," he said. "That's where I'd go if I didn't have this job."

"Shall we taxi over to Sazzae?" When they muscled into the club, everyone asked where Shintaro was. "Not here. I forgot my wallet." Tomorrow's groupies bought Maximilian and Lois a drink. He clinked glasses with Lois, whose structures he'd come to rely on for dealing with the unpredictable side of life. Day in, night out, he was more often as she depicted him in her paintings. Regal, handling everything. She painted his muscles gray, and said he was like a rock.

"There's nothing going on here," Maximilian said, back on the couch. "I've had it with work. Maybe I'll quit my job. Maybe the bank won't be there anymore. We lost a lot of money. Everything went south. All of a sudden everyone started selling the Tiki fish stock, Arnie's oil stock, his tech stock. The major players took their money off the table, and we were in too deep."

"How deep?"

"It hurts to say it."

"Come on. Who would I tell?

"Seven billion."

"Seven billion! That could feed a whole country. That's more than your trading line."

"Yeah, but I sold puts. The risk was unlimited, and it wasn't just me. The CFO and several of the boys got caught up in the insider scam and levered up the bank for a tip on fish stock."

"Can't you get us transferred to Paris?"

"I don't think they'd be as eager to see Tomorrow in Paris. Anyway, London is the financial center of Europe. "

"Then let's stay here."

"How? There's an investigation going on at the bank. I don't like being anywhere near that stuff. It's every man for himself, and they could try to pin it on me to save face for the CFO."

"How did you get involved?"

"I don't know how it started, but I found out about it when I was walking by Arnie's phone. It was ringing. What would you have done?"

"Answered the phone."

"That's what I did. I heard more than I should have, I guess. Then, I coattailed the trade. It worked out for a while, but pretty soon there were these goons standing around on the way out. "

"Did they touch you?"

"They kidnapped me. They wanted to know how much stock we had bought, and when we had soaked up enough fish stock, they stung us. They sold theirs and moved the market. That's how it is. Everybody'll tell you when to buy because they want their stock to go up, but when it's time for them to sell, they need more buyers, and you're the last to hear about it. It sunk before we could get out. I'm not worried about the Namazu. They love us now — now that we've made them seven billion. It's my colleagues who are dangerous now. They're looking for a scapegoat."

"Let's go to Paris," she said. "You're a social artist. You can make it anywhere. You have an army of friends. And the wine's better there."

They were on their way to the club. He walked down the street with her. She was safe. The earth stood still, and they walked through it. Her hand went into his like a leaf landing on the ground. She knew him. He took ladies' hands like leaf collecting. There was nothing to it. He would sit with his back to them and watch TV. He did not tell them where to go, but they eventually left. They didn't hate him. They had never known who he was.

But she, Lois, detested, for example, his love of money, even though she knew he loved to be hated for his love of money. She couldn't help being a woman on this point, and he always tried to buy women. "I hate your money." Her stomach burned as they walked down the street side by side. "I hate it."

She imagined the stones of Paris as they walked through the shanty Tokyo town. He rapped, "Lois slow slang jong, can too cantafable turn to me, me turn the table slang jong song." She looked over at him. At his thick blond hair. He was lost. Insider trading deal, huh. She'd known there was some blossoming politic. The only way to find out was not to ask. Just as the only way to hold him was to deny everything.

She followed him into Sazzae. Other men had found their way out of her heart and into her body. Not Maximilian. She wouldn't knock him down from his pedestal, and he would let her hang him on his wall. She would paint him as a cornerstone in Paris, now that she understood what was going on. Everyone at Sazzae said, hi. "Yeah, maybe Tomorrow'll come later." Maximilian and Lois ordered drinks. The groupies paid and led them over to their table, but instead of sitting down, Lois walked around the table toward Maximilian. Maximilian had walked around the table away from her. She tried to go to him again, but he kept on walking around the table. She walked around after him, faster. He went faster, too.

"I'm chasing you," she said.

"I'm chasing you," he said.

"You're following me," she said.

He had a thought and followed it off into the dark lounge. She followed him. He continued until he had crossed the room and come to the door, closed against the winter nighttime. He paced along the wall, trapped, alone. She came to him.

He turned around and took her hands and nudged her backwards. Through the door and outside they tangoed. He walked forward, she backward. He twirled her around, crossing arms. He was saying something on the stairs.

She imagined grand chandeliers. He let go of one of her hands and raised the other like a leaf. They taxied home.

Chapter 32

─────────────── ℘℘ ───────────────

Star Bright

Once Tomorrow had gotten downtown, he couldn't get a moment to himself. He sat with his makeup artist under the hot spotlights. Just as he was starting to sing, his manager came in. "We have a meeting with an Italian producer."

"When?"

"Now, in there."

Shintaro breathed deeply in his black suit jacket and went into the meeting room. They bowed and shook hands. The producer spoke English very quickly for an Italian. Shintaro could only decipher some of the words through the Italian accent.

"I love being in Japan. I have many friends in Japan," the Italian said. "Japanese people are so interesting to me. Their lifestyles, their design. Each time I come to Japan, five different friends invite me to their houses. It's difficult because I have to choose among them. . . . Last time, I stayed with a producer from Toshiba-EMI. He has a tiny apartment. He rolled out the futon, and I slept on the floor.

"I'd like to hear about Tomorrow's current activities," said the Italian. "In other areas than singing and song-writing, too. It is always interesting to select at least two arts and strive within these, in the first for competence and in the second for excellence. Excuse me for being frank, but in Italy, people are not generally impressed with Japanese singers. Italians find the Japanese commercial sound too predictable. We produced 'The Snake Charmers' from Detroit. The all-girl band with the saxophonist. Anyway. Italians don't need Japan for western imitations. We can do that ourselves. Tomorrow, however, has a unique sound and rhythm that I feel we can promote all over Europe. Perhaps he has an unusually classical Japanese upbringing?"

Shintaro sat up. The meeting would have to run itself. He bowed to his manager who was already answering the question. Shintaro excused himself and closed the door on the meeting. He walked down Aoyamadori toward the foreigners' building, went up the stairs and opened the door.

Lois was modeling the white kimono, mostly for her own sake, in front of the mirror. Maximilian had done a poor job at tying the obe behind her back, but at least she could get an idea of its general shape. Her painting wasn't too far off. It needed to be a little bit longer in back, the waist a little bit higher, as high as an ancient Roman dress. Maximilian had walked off. She turned to see him opening the door for Shintaro.

The Japanese boy's eyes widened. At last he saw *her* in the white kimono. She was like a princess.

"Do you know how to untie this in back?" she said.

Maximilian must have helped her put it on. She was like a princess, Shintaro thought, as long as she didn't open her mouth. His face flushed red.

"We had to take a picture. I want to paint the knot."

Shintaro looked out at the painting on the terrace. He recognized some of her in the new white abstraction struggling against the black square.

"Sit down," Maximilian said to Shintaro. "We've been waiting for you."

"Yes. I have been too busy. Finally, I left."

"I hope you're not missing anything important," Lois said.

"Everything is important. I have no time."

"You are the marginal of the marginal. We never see you. Come on. It's tea time." It was always tea time. They drank some tea. Shintaro had to go back to the studio. Maximilian walked him outside and then came back. "What's up with Shintaro?" Maximilian said.

"His occupation is being occupied. I don't know. I should be asking you that. I thought you had gotten bored of him."

"I know how sad he is about his grandfather, and he's still so serious about this teen idol stuff. He devotes all his time to it, but he doesn't seem to want to do it."

"I don't know," she finally said. "Japanese are funny about things like that."

"Like what? Any Japanese would kill to be in his position."

"Well Shintaro isn't like most Japanese."

"All Japanese are like most Japanese."

"He's not," she said.

Maximilian looked at her, would not stop looking at

her. "I was doing him a favor. He's almost angry about it."

"Don't worry. He'll be fine," she said. "He's got some hang-ups."

"Like what exactly?"

"It's difficult to explain."

He glared at her.

"Lack of self-confidence. He thinks he's profane."

"What? Profane? O.K. I'm not worried about it anymore."

The phone rang. Lois shuffled across the room in the narrow kimono. "It's for you," she said.

"Who is it?" Maximilian asked.

"A man."

"Tell him I'm in London."

She shuffled back into the library. "He's in London," she said into the phone.

Maximilian was sitting on the couch staring out the window. Something was not right, Lois thought. She had never seen him so completely distracted.

"I'm going to Korea," he said.

"Okay," she said.

"I have to do some paperwork for my visa."

"Sure." She knew that he didn't have to bother with paperwork. His company took care of him like a Siamese cat. Only gypsies like her had to leave to extend their visas. Now he would leave her to run his errands. "What is it?"

"It's so tight, it's under my skin."

"What?"

"Nothing. I won't be long. Just stay here and answer the phone."

"Sounds dangerous," she said.

"Don't worry about me."

"I meant for me."

"There's no free lunch, partner," he said.

He was gone when she woke up the next morning. The phone was ringing. She was shocked. They usually didn't bother her when Maximilian wasn't there. She picked up the receiver. "Hello," said a Japanese man. "I want to talk to Jack."

"He isn't here," Lois said.

"Are you there alone?" he said.

"No," she lied. "Who is this?"

"Who are you there with?"

She froze.

"You are alone." The man laughed and hung up the phone.

She began to feel a familiar premonition, as strong as when her uncle had announced that Maximilian was moving out of the house. They never saw him again. He might be dead. She thought of not leaving the house. She picked up the mystery novel which had fallen off a pile of books. There was a strange gravitational pull; her signet ring had slipped off last night in the bathtub as Maximilian was packing to leave. There were other warnings. Her mother had taken to warning her of things after Maximilian had left their household: that if Lois didn't stop leading all those men on, one of them would kill her. That sort of thing seemed very possible at the moment.

She decided to leave some evidence of her whereabouts in her room. After all, no one from the U.S. knew that she lived here with Maximilian and Shintaro.

The phone rang again. She didn't answer it. It would be safer outside, at least until Shintaro got home. She locked the door and went out. The shops were open, even on Sunday. She passed a stand full of yellow socks for 300 yen. Her favorite color. Another opportunity to leave a trace. Her guardian angel? She decided to leave a trace, asking for directions to Shintaro's studio as she bought the socks, just in case the police inquired around the location of her last business transaction for the whereabouts of the missing girl. Funny, the shopkeeper actually asked her to sign their mailing list. Lois explained that she was American and had two addresses, and she wrote both. She was scared.

Fear sharpens the senses. She wanted to go back home, and remembered she had felt the opposite way when they separated as children. As children, it was, if only I could have gone with him. This time, she had put the idea of following him out of her mind and watched him go. And it was the same, going, staying: she had no control over the outcome. She didn't know if the error was in the past or in what she was about to do to correct it. She seemed to get everything she asked for, and lose everything. She had been offered so many chances to retrieve Maximilian. Did she always take him in? Did it ever happen that he didn't win? This ritual would go on, always unfinished as long as she lived. He would never die.

There was no time left, she thought, as she stepped out into the street. She needed a strategy if she was going to stand a chance. Fighter, fighter.

"Hey sister." A dark green car pulled up and drove

slowly along the sidewalk. "Need a lift? It's cold and I love Jesus. He was my sister."

Her blood slowed. Things like this never happened in Tokyo. Without looking at the driver, she went into a shop. She walked down the aisles, lost amidst suppositions about Maximilian. The strange telephone call nagged her. He was involved in something shady. He was not who he said he was. He seemed so lazy, but he was in excellent shape. He moved his moped two inches as if landing a plane. He arrived at a stop light as if descending on a target. He was too normal. The businessman story fit like a shadow. She observed his shadow; she painted his shadow, but not the picture. There was the mail for another person that he received. And he talked a lot about the truth, too. He demanded the truth from her, as if she owed it to him. A sophisticated form of rape: especially the non-sexual aspect. Unless he had a mission. Perhaps he demanded the truth of her because he needed to know that she was not a spy, or needed to know exactly who she was. "You didn't exactly tell the truth about Shintaro," he'd said.

They were at Sazzae, the first time they'd met. He wouldn't tell her his name because she wouldn't tell him where she was from. "You think I'm deceiving you," she'd said, "but I don't think so. Why are people obliged to reveal everything the first time they meet a stranger? Do you have so little respect for other people that you think you can just arrive and demand the truth as if they owed it to you? Never mind making them comfortable." She could still see his corn-dog smile. She didn't smile. He understood that argument a little too easily, as if he had started to feel guilty about not revealing his true identity, and wanted to know if Lois would hold it against him one day when she found out. Truthfulness and shreds of facts were different things. She knew how he felt about the truth. He was Maximilian.

Her heels clicked on the pavement outside of the studio. She felt Maximilian's presence. Maybe he was thinking about her at that moment. Maybe he had a good reason for secrecy. They were both Americans, and Americans are innocent until proven guilty. He was endangering her by withholding the facts. Maybe it wasn't she who was directly in danger. Maybe it was someone in her family, or someone so close to her that she could feel the danger, like a limb being severed. He had spoken to her on an emotional level. He had touched her, was her friend. Hers. If it was Maximilian who was in danger, he was the only one with enough facts to figure out a strategy. She changed her strategy. She would tell him the facts, and demand the truth.

She asked for Shintaro at the studio. They made her wait a long time. Then he was there.

"Hello," he said.

"Hi."

"Hello," he said again, his lips close to hers.

"How are you?"

"Fine. What are you doing?"

"Nothing. I'm free. Maximilian has gone to Korea."

He smelled her hair. She sounded scared. It made him nervous, too.

"I was wondering if you wanted to come home for lunch."

"Yes. I'm finished here."

Shintaro walked her back to the apartment. They had lunch alone by the window. She looked out on her self-composing painting. It seemed to have a kind of soul of its own. It was progressing on its own built-in evolutionary trajectory toward a logical point of completion. It was a ritual, the sacrificial canvas for a more ancient purpose, before beauty, when art was a prayer, an incantation. When a rain dance was for rain. She felt like she was being watched, and tried to look at herself in the beginning. She had started painting wooly beasts on cave walls to pray for a successful hunt and was continuing on a long trip, never knowing if her art had dictated the outcome. If only she were more aware. There was something she couldn't see. Wasn't that always the problem? There was something missing; the object was not the subject. She was shaking.

He didn't ask her to explain. They had finished lunch in silence. The earth trembled. "I don't like it when that happens," Lois said.

"Don't be afraid," Shintaro said. "The Japanese folktale say that is the *Namazu*. The earthquake fish. He wiggle under the sea and causes the earth to shake."

She laughed and moved closer to him.

He took her onto his lap and tugged at her clothes until she was naked. Afterward, he watched her sleeping and worried that she would get cold. He was her blanket. Her eyes fluttered open. "Maximilian's not easy to understand," Shintaro said cautiously. "Maybe you are not safe here."

"That's ridiculous," she could say, now that he was here to protect her. She was not a coward. "I'm fine here."

He went on kissing her as if they'd said nothing. The phone rang. Shintaro answered it. "He's in London." The afternoon wore on. The phone rang again, and she unplugged it. They watched a movie and fell asleep on the couch. At ten p.m., Lois half woke up and tried to get comfortable. She had wriggled into Shintaro's arms. He pretended to still be sleeping. His body stiffened. He let her lie there against his chest. He watched her sleep. She was like a child.

Shintaro was holding a big child. It was not so surprising after all. He was upsetting the order of things, stepping out of his place. The lowest of the low. His people were known for escape, for getting mixed up with society, forgetting their places, working for the government, marrying the wrong daughters, disgracing whole companies until that fateful day when they were discovered. There were many ways to hide, many ways to disappear. His father must have found one, somewhere, touchable.

Shintaro had never brought a friend home to his house, until Lois. She was beautiful, and let him touch her, despite everything. He stroked her hair. He had never trusted anyone, in order not to be sent back to a *buraku*. He had never had a friend, until Lois. She opened her eyes. He kissed her. She was kissing him.

Maximilian loosened his yellow tie and entered the night store with his carry-on suitcase in search of *chuhai*. He had come to terms with the fact that he couldn't stay away from Shintaro another day. He knew exactly what to say, exactly what Shintaro would say. It made perfect sense to him as he went over it again with his twisted logic. He anticipated the cocktail together with Shintaro and skimmed down the rice cracker isle. After spending the past week acquiring a suitcase full of trendy garbage, he was looked forward to modeling some of it for them. He let himself daydream of feeding his soul. Soybeans would be nice with *chuhai*. Shintaro knew how to cook these.

Metal scratched the lock. Lois' back arched in fear. There was a thud on the doorstep. The door swung open. Maximilian with a case of *chuhai* and mixer balanced on the curve of his arm.

Lois felt a wave of relief before she realized that she was naked. The fear returned. Shintaro grabbed their clothes.

Maximilian saw what he had been avoiding since the beginning. There, together on his couch. Disgusting. He dropped the *chuhai*. They jumped up and covered themselves. At first none of them spoke. The words stuck in Maximilian's throat. "This is MY place," Maximilian said.

Shintaro sat up, pointedly avoiding the American eyes. Lois stood up and found herself amidst a sudden rush of hands and booze. Maximilian smacked her face.

"I will go," Shintaro said.

"No, you stay," Maximilian said. "Lois, you go."

"Over my dead body," Lois said. She stood between Maximilian and Shintaro, and then collapsed on the floor.

Shintaro propped her feet up and tried to wake her up. Maximilian pushed him away from her. Maximilian smelled like alcohol. "If I could change every second of our mutual . . . our mutuality. You don't have honor."

Maximilian, who had sunken into cowardice and violence, picked up a bottle of *chuhai.*

"Where are you going?" Shintaro said.

"I'm not going anywhere. I'm leaving." Maximilian slammed the door and ran down the stairs. "Parasites." His thoughts raced as he picked apart the vision of the two of them, competing vultures. He remembered it at varying degrees of disintegration. *My reason for living was a delusion.* He just wanted to go to sleep in his bed. "Fine." He got into a taxi.

Shintaro and Lois lay there on the floor.

The morning light filtered through the Venetian blinds. Her body slipped away through the paper door. Shintaro heard her through the paper.

"Let's go outside," she said.

Outside? Where were his sunglasses? He pulled the couch pillow over his head. The phone rang. "Don't answer it," he said.

"Hello," she said.

The rain beat its way through the ground. It was rainy season. It hit the leaves and made the air cool and fresh. Wet dawn, ions in the air. Shintaro sat up from the couch. He saw Lois' silhouette, frozen, clenching the phone.

"Okay," she said, and hung up. She didn't move. "I'm going out," she said.

She got her coat and shoes. He put on his clothes. "What is it?" he said.

"Maximilian. I don't know. Trouble. I have to go to Shinjuku. My King Department Store. I think someone's following him."

"You think?"

"I know."

Chapter 33

───────────ಐ ೞ───────────

Blue

The playground. Time passed with a rake. Maximilian looked around, and still, no one was there. The red sun hung over Japan. A whole note in the telephone lines. Endless wires and terrace bars, and still no one but you. The wind blows through my dead heart and scatters a name on the path. Look, a fallen idol, lost name strewn on the path.

Gazing at the sky, he was young and beautiful as ever. Maximilian blue, in the middle of his courtyard, this playground, that morning, to ignore the root of his entanglement, that morning, despite the cold. A handsome young gentleman skillfully unlearning the guiding principles of *galanterie* as he wrapped his full-length punk-rock black leather jacket tighter around his bleeding chest. It was early morning. He was feeling bluer than blue, and the sand was wet.

He gazed at the branches above. As their bare fingers reached bone after bone ever upward into the fog, they also reached downward into the narrowing finitude of a knavish sensibility. He lay looking up at nothing, nothing, and the Holy Ghost. Beautiful, with your back to the world. The wind whistled through the trees, *Maximilian.*

Who knew something then. He dreamt while looking at the sky. He'd had friends and kept something of them. A falcon's pointed body had pierced the rain-begetting clouds. The song had changed, would change again. He remembered he had been writing a letter to Shintaro. He took it out of his pocket and tried to re-read it. It ended so many ways he couldn't commit himself to finishing it.

Had a soul come upon a man? So many people believe such things, they must be true. Maximilian stood in the undiscovered future. He put the unfinished letter back into his pocket and took a step. He was sad. He had been here before. But now the light had withdrawn from the alleys. He was getting closer to where he had to be. He looked at the sinking sun.

It is no rare occurrence. He had broken with his sordid past, had completely forgotten about, for example, the money he should have paid to keep from being dragged into underworld designs, about which he knew nothing, really, knee-deep in fish stock, although he was grateful she had called him an emperor. Now he drifted through the empty red taint of dawn.

They belong together, my friends. There was the red lady, "White trash." Maybe she *was* pretty. Lo! But he'd never tell her that. She wasn't Shintaro. Sacred three, etched in the sky of his heart where soon nothing would come to pass. He had come to this. Now look what they've done. Endless sky, blue with no beginning, answering only to the wind.

Chapter 34

—————————— ℰℴℭℛ ——————————

All the Queen's Men

There's something I can't see, Lois thought. I feel something missing. What? What? It was as hard as concrete. The subway station at Shinjuku Gyonemae was one dark long hallway. Water dripped down from the ceiling and formed a puddle by the tracks. An ad for Suntory whisky hung warped on the wall in back of Lois. Her hands were warm inside her white muff. Her natural tendency was to search out models to paint. Objects. Tools. Where was her *objet?* She looked. There had to be something more. He was missing.

The man, no doubt the man who had been following Maximilian these past weeks, whom Maximilian had been avoiding these past weeks, appeared on the opposite side of the tracks. He waited there a few minutes, watching Lois. She left the tracks and waited at the department store. Something was missing. No sign of Maximilian. He might be at Sazzae.

She phoned his office from a coffee shop. "No, he didn't come in today." She would go to Sazzae.

The black door was locked. She banged on it with both fists. Too late. She went to a coffee shop and called. The phone call was forwarded and continued ringing in a heavier tone. "Yes, I saw him," Masami told her, "but he left with some men."

"What men?" she demanded. "Where?"

"I don't know, maybe they went for a walk in the park."

"A walk!" She was on her way to the park to find Maximilian.

He consumed her. He knew it. Down to her ends, like a ring of fire. He liked being her tool, her *objet*. Where?

In darkness except for a white pinprick of light, a distant star, confusing, the violence. Reduced again. Tiny soul, not even a child. Shivering soul. There is the white star, but there is also life. Back to the world that has recoiled. Too hard to bear.

Maximilian! She, disoriented without Maximilian, walked through the trees toward the maze. He was beyond her. He must be somewhere. Her way of looking must be wrong; the trees were strange. Nothing had a name in Japan. Maximilian. She stopped at the end of the maze. There was a police car. She ducked back and peeked through the hedge.

The water in the fountain tumbled, red, from tier to tier. It had happened. The policemen made notes. She prayed that it wasn't Maximilian, lying face down in the red water. They were in no hurry to drag him out. One of the policemen made the sign of the cross. Another policeman pulled an envelope out of his jacket pocket.

"Maximilian!"

The policemen looked up. She ran back through the maze of hedges away from the policemen.

Shintaro was waiting for her on the steps of the apartment building. His face was a mirror: grave. It began to rain again. He lit two cigarettes between the drops, and handed one to her. "He's dead," she said.

"Dead?!"

The smoking two, two abysses, stepped into the street. They walked through the grey rain. It was raining, they noticed, as Shintaro tried to re-light Lois' cigarette. "Where do you think he went?"

"The Champs Elysées."

They passed through the wet streets, not saying anything. It was not good. It would be a long time before anything would be good. They were keeping quiet at every chance. They walked and smoked and concentrated hard to keep the quiet. They pretended to walk on as before, side by side, never touching, always walking, always smoking, always concentrated on their parallel ways through the abysmal streets.

They were soaked. They ran up to a coffee shop. He opened the door for her. She opened the next door for him. They bought two more packs of cigarettes which tasted worse, but also better now that they would go on walking together, for a while. "They found a letter in Maximilian's pocket," she said.

They looked at each other, about to say something, and went out. He opened the first and the second door for her.

"You must disappear," she said. It was getting dark. "I'm leaving, too."

His face hardened, her words carved on him.

"I'm going," she said again.

"Where?"

"I don't know. I'm tired. It hurts. Someplace beautiful. Look, just don't go back to the house."

"I won't."

"Goodbye."

He bowed.

She walked away.

He stood there for a moment. He wandered down the street after her. But she had turned off somewhere. He walked alone down the street.

Silent avalanche.
I — a footstep: summer-snow —
Did not hear you go.

He could not feel his generations behind him now. He was not one of the untouchables, but a severed soul. A sponge in the world's mouth. The streets filled up with people, and he soaked up all the misery, hurt, disgrace, like an angel in hell. He had to go on.

Chapter 35

―――――――――୫ාC୫―――――――――

Nooze

The story appeared on the front page of the newspaper. The police were looking for the famous teen idol Tomorrow. Murder suspect was in the first paragraph, but the headline read, "Teen Idol Untouchable." That alone would have killed Taro if he weren't already dead. Shintaro put the paper down. Where was Lois? Had she slept outside?

They'd picked her up as she'd turned the corner, one street over from Shintaro. They put her in the police car. She was not crying when they picked her up. She had cried for him often throughout her life. Now it was too late.

She brought the white muff. They put her into the car and drove her through rush hour. She stared out the window, not seeing anything, except when they passed Sazzae.

They asked her many questions at the police station.

Did she live with Maximilian? Who else lived there?

"Why?" she asked. "Kill the killers, and then what? Do you think that a death is mathematical?"

They hammered on. What was Maximilian's involvement with the Japanese mafia? "Maximilian was not involved with the Yakuza." How long had she known Maximilian and Shintaro? Why did she follow him to the park? Did she know anything about this letter?

Lois took the letter in her shaking hands. A love letter? She read it. It was the ultimate love letter. It was a will. Maximilian had left Shintaro one million dollars in a bank account in Paris. The letter fell to the linoleum floor of the police station. "He loves Shintaro," she said. "Another one of life's little jokes." The four officers discussed the letter among themselves, and then looked at her for an explanation. "Explanation?" The earth tore open and swallowed him up. It ripped him out and cast him in the past. "I don't know," she said, "why he has chosen this path. To avoid pain. I don't think he's lost." Someone brought her a cup of coffee. She sat up. "A shattering of the present."

The police found a purple scarf at the scene of the accident. "Do you know anything about this?"

"I don't recognize it. I hope you don't suspect me. Really. What percentage of murders are committed by women?"

"Ten. However, not only women wear women's clothes. Our job is to narrow it down."

Lois, as if in her white kimono, looked out the window, the black square having swallowed her king. Did *she* make it rain? Rainy season had come here many times. She looked out at the water running down the window, enough rain to fill a sea. Space graphed itself out on the open sea, where time was nothing more than a million points of afternoon light, electric on the blue horizon. The sea signaled the sky: a million points of sunlight flashed toward the horizon.

"I always felt like I could have done more, except staring into a sea. What can I do about a dead friend? Let go? Outrageous. I could never let them change without remark. Possess and let go, the final criticism. I will not engage in this dismissal."

"I predicted all of this in my paintings." She listened to the waves, the first day at sea, and put a stroke on the canvass. She listened to the waves and knew that he would never die.

"Seize the paintings," said the officer over his shoulder. "Investigate them for clues." The police officer turned back to Lois. "Go on."

Outrage. No thought of going into the white light, though it was approaching, soothing and growing larger. Outrage, must get back. There were other lives to live. Go into the nearest one. Resist the white light. In need of a body. Corporeal tension. Life.

"Maximilian came and went as he pleased. I could still hear his voice the way it had sounded two years ago piping through the radiator from the floor below. His voice came through the walls, although it was only his answering machine. He was networking. At Harvard, already doing business, Maximilian. It was September, a new school year. I was trying to concentrate on Plato. I heard a door slam down below. He must have been walking across the room, putting his books down. He played back the whole half-hour of messages. I knelt down on the floor next to my desk and pressed my ear against the cool radiator." She looked around the room. She felt him near her now.

"He had to be one of those excruciatingly normal types, even though everyone at Harvard was strange in some way. He put on a top forty tape. I'd known it. I banged on the radiator. How were we going to make it through the year with that racket going on? A few weeks later, whenever I banged on the radiator, the phone rang immediately. 'Can I come up?' and then the knock, followed by a game of chess, which Maximilian always won, which was his problem. He could barely get me to rest in his arms."

"How the tables had turned in Tokyo. I'd taken his bet, and he won the game, won again, simply dropping out of life. He was mine, and now I'm his. And we are free."

The sea graphed itself out, a stark undulation beneath the haphazard clouds. The waves rose like voices out of the past. A million points of pale light flashing out toward the grey horizon. It was different. It is impossible for you to understand how it was before Tokyo.

When she stopped, the police urged her to go on. They kept on taking notes when they didn't understand her. She no longer cared whether or not she made sense. The only thing was to talk. She and Maximilian had met at school, but she knew him before that, too.

"How is that?"

"How?" It was a long time ago in the black painted valleys, so low down in the depths of everything that daylight never touched them. There it was decided that the crown should be bestowed upon the Archduke Maximilian, by popular election. Then the assassins came, for political reasons. "The politics of brutality, I think. You have to look in the valleys. The great will climb from the depths. But you didn't answer *my* question. Do you think death is mathematical? Does it add up?"

The policemen looked at each other.

"You will understand when you see my paintings. Out of the darkness comes a lady in a white dress. She's white, and a dark square rests at the lady's feet, the gate, which is also a man, Maximilian, the Emperor. In front of the gate that is Maximilian is an orderly garden. Everything seems disconnected without respect to form. That's why Maximilian devoted himself to writing a tomb on courtly etiquette. He was gentle, even though everything was disconnected, not on intersecting planes. It was a shock, seeing Maximilian again after he'd been gone for so long." Lois searched their stone faces. Doubt. "It was time to close the embassy and go to Paris. To convince Napoleon."

Nevertheless, a policeman wrote down what she said. "What happened when you met Maximilian at school?"

"It was hard to get over the shock. He saw that and helped me."

"The shock of meeting Maximilian again?"

Maximilian was there and then gone, like everything inside of her that had never died. "Yes." When she saw him again, she would yell at him. Never die!

"What happened next?"

She composed herself. "That year I was in a magazine. They asked us to pose for it. Be in the magazine. Maximilian was very free-thinking. And he didn't mind if I did it. I mean it was O.K. with him, to pose nude."

"You?"

"Why not? Yes. I did it."

"How much did they pay?"

"I didn't hear anything about it for a long time. I forgot about it. I left the lecture hall on the last day of the school year, junior year. I threw my stuff into a taxi fast. I closed my eyes on one world and opened them onto another where consequences didn't apply."

"Japan."

"Yes, a fresh start. But never without Maximilian. 'As a reminder, you've boarded flight seventy-five with non-stop service to Detroit.'"

Corpus. Novum. Into the black. The memory of gravity, of events from long ago, many lives, such sorrow, it seemed now all so painful, to be severed many times brutally from life by other living flesh. Now look what they've done. Now look what they've done.

Lois remembered how the stewardess had swished past. Her fragrance lingered: female, tight. A voice came across the loudspeaker: "Maximilian paging Lois Coffin. Please come to the front of the airplane." Not like the dull soft male cologne smell, but something you'd want to penetrate.

Through the black. Earth. The clouds above mankind. Technology. Civilization in flight. Airplane. Must not let it end this way. Never. Never. Never die.

"It reminded me of Regina. Of the Detroit queen. I

followed her to the front of the airplane. Maximilian was asking for a coffin way back then. We have to get him out of the morgue and into a coffin!"

The policeman stopped writing. "We will. Do you like men?"

"Do I like men? We were on Nantucket. Flute, guitar, wine, fire, red moon, the sky went orange, and black. I tried to bring him back through my art: through incantation. Then there were the waves crashing onto the shore until dawn. The waves crashed. A morning swim, his soft long embrace and dark curls as I savored his body in the ocean spray more as time grew less until the irrefutable end: he was out of time; I was running to the plane."

Now look what they've done.

"I made it, the last person on board. The luckiest, they must have thought watching me breeze into my seat at the last minute. I hurt. Flight seventy-five to Detroit. I looked out on the ocean and cried. I missed him so much."

"You said you remember meeting Jack in Detroit?"

She remembered meeting Maximilian in Detroit. She remembered meeting Maximilian at Harvard, on the Champs Elysées. In her Latin class. He climbed in through her window. When she asked him where he was from, he said Leningrad, he said, Bucharest, Corsica. He was playing in a café when she met him. "Yes."

A familiar physique in a long-sleeved police uniform walked through the hallway outside of the glass window. As he went out the door, he turned his profile. Masami!

"Tell us about Detroit."

She sat there stunned. Could the police be working for the Yakuza? Could Maximilian and Masami have been working for the police?

"And?" Light blue sleeves covered the police officer's arms. There was no sign of a tattoo on his neck, either.

"I . . . I was going to Detroit. I flew back to Regina and the graduates of the school of hard knocks. All my CDs were there in Detroit. It was my body, and that was that. Maximilian loved my body. Sex was not sexist. I went over to the newsstand and bought the magazine. I opened it to my face, me, hardly any clothes. I said, 'I'm in trouble.' I thought I was. Back in Detroit, they would not understand female freedom. Where would they? 'In heaven,' Maximilian had said. I *hadn't* fallen victim to a conspiracy. Their morality was built-in. I was angry at Maximilian, and he was angry at me. He told me, 'Now I understand why you took four years of Latin.'"

"Next day, Javier's porch, Cass Corridor. Punks barbecuing. Flat beer: Coors. There was a boycott on Coors. Coors was on sale. No one had seen the magazine. Rap music was coming from one of the cars. Regina was dancing on the steps. We were porch monkeys. Tiny Elton was wearing a leather jacket for the first time. He pulled up in a truck full of vacuum cleaners to sell with his sister, who was pregnant. 'Now remember, when it starts to get tight, we go back to the baby and then hit them with the trip to Florida.'"

"'Jesus, it's coming!' I said.

"Everyone laughed.

"'Been going door to door?' Javier asked.

"'Yeah.' Elton got himself a beer. He told me Regina had been spreading rumors about him and me. Perfect timing. My appetite went the way of my reputation, and I managed to get drunk quietly on the steps."

"I woke up at five a.m. and couldn't fall back asleep. Elton had said Regina had been spreading rumors about me. *Et tu Brutus?* Women stick together. 'Regina, damn it, wake up,' I said.

"'What?' Regina said in her guilty voice. I could always tell when she was lying. 'Look,' I said, and opened the magazine to my page.

"Regina looked at it. 'Oh my,' she feigned, 'You mean everything we've been saying about you is true?'

"'This is not funny.'

"'What did Maximilian say?'

"'He hasn't seen it, but he was there when I did it. He thinks I'm free to do what I want.'

"'There ain't too many men like that.'

"'Yeah,' I said. 'Maybe he isn't like that.' I had left for summer vacation without saying goodbye. I decided to call him on the East Coast. It was the middle of the night. He answered the phone. He said he was constantly thinking I was about to call.

"'You could have called me,' I said.

"He said he'd thrown out my address and phone number.

"I offered to give it to him again if he promised not to throw it out.

"'I won't throw it out, but you know what I'll do? I'll pick up the phone and dial the first few numbers, and hang up.'

"'O.K., then I'll just give you the first few numbers. Got a pen?'

"'Yeah, give me the first nine.'

"He was such a baby then. Everything touched him. I could still touch him.

"Then school started, and Maximilian came knocking on my door. He was always there. Ever since I was a child."

"A child."

"Yes."

The policeman closed his notebook and conferred with his colleagues. After some time, they came back. "We were looking for something a little more conclusive."

She brushed back her hair and zipped up her coat. "Is it my fault if death is not conclusive?"

After conferring among themselves, they offered to drive her home. "No, I'm O.K.," she said.

They looked at her doubtfully. "I don't know how much the dead man himself meant to you," said the policeman, "but just to let you know, there is not conclusive evidence enough to show anything. For us, this was just another drunken suicide. Maybe you don't know Maximilian very well. This letter we found in his pocket is a love letter marked, 'Shintaro'. It seems you have confused the dead man with someone else."

She looked out at the sea, undulating, stark beneath the clouds. Sometimes someone says something to you, and you don't hear it until months later. "No, I have not confused the dead man with someone else," she said walking through the Tuileries months later. The waves rose like voices out of the past.

Chapter 36

―――――――――――ᏕᎧᏟᎡ―――――――――――

Architecture of a Soul

Paris is heaven in the month of June with its infinite structure. The walls of the buildings on the rue Fabre d'Eglantine repeat an architecture of souls, tombstones beseeching Napoleon.

Now Shintaro knew the hardness of the world. He fingered the ironic wad of bills in his pocket, more money than he had ever dreamed of, and drifted down the street like a leaf. Onto the steps of the Gare du Lyon whose cement floor glistened under the skylights above the quays. Morning streamed down from the skylights onto the protest of the marching metropolis that dissipated in all directions like an *avant garde* ballet. Life-like. He wondered if he had woken up. She would find him here. He stirred his coffee and looked across the tracks. He waited.

At midnight in Paris, there was an apocalyptic fog on the Seine, and a floodlit Ferris wheel to visit in the Tuileries. Shintaro bought another ticket and got into the seat alone. As the Ferris wheel turned, it projected gigantic shadows floating up into the rooftop apartments. On the way down, he rippled through the immortal stones, tombstones housing generations of ancient jealousies. They refused to part, and instead sculpted the living cell tissue they encroached.

Tiny soul in search of a man. In darkness except for a white pinprick of light, confusing, the violence. There's the white star, but there is also life. The world, wide awake, and there, Shintaro nearby. Back to the world that recoiled on me!

The Ferris wheel tossed Shintaro up to the clouds. He waited for the sky to crack open, sensed the reassuring presence and knew that someone was joining him.

Together. Overwhelming security.

Our shadow mingled with the stones as it traveled down the building cliffs to the river. The ground skidded by. We held our breath. There she was — Lo! — on the riverbank below.

Bronze hands gripping the Ferris wheel, Maximilian mounted the city again.

About the Author

J. L. Morin grew up in inner-city Detroit. Morin wrote *Sazzae* as a creative thesis toward a bachelor's degree at Harvard ('86-'87), followed by three novels for future publication: *Traveling Light; Polis;* and *Trickster of Phraxos.* Morin has had fiction published in *Above Ground: An Anthology of Living Fiction, The Harvard Advocate* and *Harvard Yisei,* and articles and translations in *The Detroit News, Agence France Presse, Livonia Observer Eccentric Newspapers,* and *The Harvard Crimson.*

J. L. Morin traded derivatives in New York for six years while studying nights at New York University's Stern School of Business (MBA '97). Morin's experience includes working for the Federal Reserve Bank posted to the 107th floor of the World Trade Center, working as a TV newscaster on an island in the Mediterranean, as adjunct faculty at Boston University, and as a diplomatic spouse. Contact: jlmorin@post.harvard.edu